THE COUNCIL'S DECISION

"Ladies and gentlemen," Kirk said, raising his glass. "To peace across the universe."

Jon smiled broadly. "Yes indeed," he said. "Peace by all means. Peace by *any* means."

Kirk tipped his glass in reply, drained it as they did. "You sent for us," he said. "Therefore you must have some knowledge of the United Federation of Planets and the advantages to aligning yourselves with us."

Jon nodded. "We do have some limited technology. Not that we're backward, by any means, but we're not nearly as advanced as you."

"I'm sure your technology could benefit greatly from association with the Federation."

"Possibly," said Jon. "But that decision does not rest with us."

"No?" asked Kirk, surprised.

"The Council is concerned more in the day-to-day affairs of the planet. Ultimate responsibility for a long-reaching decision of this sort would of course rest with Captain Perry."

"Captain Wayne Perry?" asked Kirk incredulously.

"Of course," said Jon. "He brought us here from the stars. All major decisions are referred to him. He should be along shortly."

Kirk looked at Spock in amazement. Wayne Perry had been the captain of the colonists' ship. If this was true, he would be over *three hundred* years old!

"We look forward to meeting Captain Perry," said Spock. It was a typical Vulcan understatement.

PERRY'S PLANET

A Star Trek™ Novel

by Jack C. Haldeman II

BANTAM BOOKS
TORONTO • NEW YORK • LONDON • SYDNEY • AUCKLAND

PERRY'S PLANET
A Bantam Book / February 1980
2nd printing . . . March 1980
3rd printing . . . September 1984

Star Trek is a trademark of Paramount Pictures Corporation.
Registered in the United States patent and trademark office.

ISBN 0-553-24193-1

Published simultaneously in the United States and Canada

Bantam Books are published by Bantam Books, Inc. Its trade-
mark, consisting of the words "Bantam Books" and the por-
trayal of a rooster, is Registered in U.S. Patent and Trademark
Office and in other countries. Marca Registrada. Bantam
Books, Inc., 666 Fifth Avenue, New York, New York 10103.

PRINTED IN THE UNITED STATES OF AMERICA

H   12 11 10 9 8 7 6 5 4 3

For Alice Lorena and Jennifer Sarah.
Good kids.

PERRY'S
PLANET

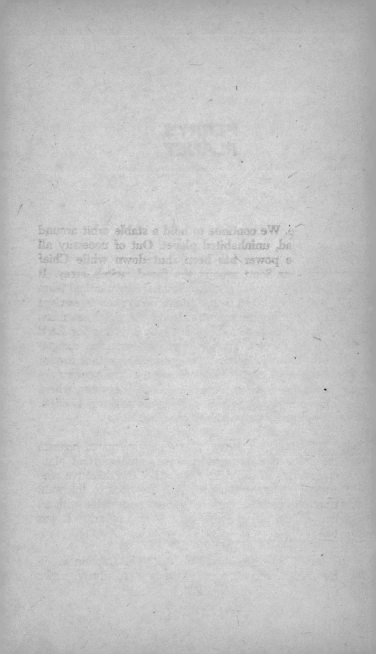

CHAPTER ONE

Captain's Log, Stardate 6827.3:

Update. We continue to hold a stable orbit around the dead, uninhabited planet. Out of necessity all impulse power has been shut down while Chief Engineer Scott repairs the fused switch array. It should not delay us much longer. The medical team we are carrying to the planet Waycross is anxious to continue. So are we. This is the third extension on our mission and we are long overdue for R&R at Starbase 6. The dilithium crystals are dangerously low, in need of replenishing, but that cannot be helped at this time. As soon as the repairs are completed, we will continue on to Waycross, where the medical team and supplies are urgently needed. From there we will head for Starbase 6.

The unnamed orange planet slowly rotated beneath the Starship *Enterprise*. It wasn't an important planet, just one in the right place. Like the detective who always sat facing the door with his back to the wall, Captain James T. Kirk felt more comfortable with an uninhabited planet at his back. It was security. It was habit.

"Engineerin' to Bridge."

"Kirk here. Go ahead, Scotty." The Captain sat in his chair, relaxed, alert. It was a relatively minor problem, an easy repair job. A nuisance, nonetheless. Still, things seemed to be well under control.

"I've got the pesky switches fixed now, sir. I dinna' think they'll be givin' us any more trooble."

"The old chewing gum and coat hanger trick again, Scotty?" asked Kirk with a grin.

"Beggin' yer pardon, sir. I dinna' understan'."

"Nothing, Scotty. Just an old-fashioned cure-all."

"I assure you there's nothin' auld-fashioned back here, sir." He sounded genuinely hurt.

"I'm sure of that, Scotty. Good job. Carry on."

"Aye, sir."

Kirk looked around the bridge. Everything was in order. "Prepare to leave orbit," he said.

"Aye, sir," said Sulu, moving forward to enter the proper coordinates.

Spock leaned back from his screen, turned toward Kirk with a puzzled look on his face. "Captain," he said. "There is something very strange here. I'm getting a reading where—"

The great bulk of the starship suddenly slipped sideways and gave a sickening roller-coaster dip. Alarms clanged throughout the ship. *"Red alert!" "All decks, red alert!"* The lights flickered, dimmed, went out entirely for a second, were replaced by the softer lights of the emergency power. *"Battle stations! We are under attack!"*

The sharp, angry lines of a Klingon warship appeared on the screen in front of them. It hadn't been there a few seconds ago. Blasts of pure energy leaped from the ship. The *Enterprise*, now with full deflectors, rocked slightly under each impact.

"Activate the main phaser banks," said Kirk.

"Locked in on target, sir," said Sulu, hunched tensely over his controls.

"Fire."

A burst of phaser fire spit out from the *Enterprise*

2

and lapped against the enemy ship. It rocked unsteadily, retreated.

Kirk released his rigid grip on the arms of his chair. "Damage report," he barked.

The intercom was a babble of voices, some calm, most excited. Kirk picked out Engineering.

"Scott here, sir. We took a bad one just below us, verra bad. Casualties, canna' say how many. We're turnin' aboot 3/4 power, most of it's goin' to maintain the deflectors. The dilithium crystals, sir—"

"I know all about the crystals, Scotty. Do what you can."

"Aye, sir."

Other stations reported in. They had taken one solid hit. It had done considerable damage, but the deflectors were holding.

"Captain, the ship is changing course. It seems to be heading for the other side of the planet."

Kirk nodded. That would make sense. Even partially disabled, the *Enterprise* was no sitting duck, not by a long shot. The Klingon vessel would use the planet as a shield. Having lost the element of surprise, the enemy ship wouldn't be taking any more chances than necessary.

"Keep the planet between us, Mr. Sulu. We have repairs to make. Maintain red alert."

"Aye, Captain."

"Spock. What happened?"

"A very curious thing, Captain. I received an apparent sensor reading just before we were attacked, but the reading I had indicated a much smaller mass and an entirely different direction. There was no warning of the Klingon vessel at all."

"Your opinion?"

"Based on the extremely limited facts at our disposal, Captain, it would appear that the Klingon ship is equipped with a device that we are unfamiliar with. It managed to fool our sensors, feed through faulty data, and slip in undetected. That allowed them time to fire one shot before our deflectors automatically erected. A check on our sensor network shows everything operational, there is no readily apparent malfunction in that system. By some unknown means they were able to approach us undetected until it was almost too late."

"If we were to capture that Klingon ship, Mr. Spock, what do you think our chances would be of discovering how they evaded our sensors?"

"The chances would be very good, Captain, approaching certainty," said Spock. "But we have our orders. They are quite explicit."

"I know the orders very well, Mr. Spock," said Kirk a little too abruptly. "I was simply thinking out loud."

Lieutenant Uhura twisted in her chair, head cocked, hand to her earpiece. "Captain. I have a transmission coming in from the Klingon ship."

"Put it through, Lieutenant."

The planet on the screen faded and was replaced by the face of a male Klingon officer. The face was vaguely familiar. His smile was forced, eyes cold as ice. A scar traced a thin line across his forehead. Behind him, at rigid attention, stood two Klingon officers of lesser rank.

"We finally meet, Captain James Kirk."

"Do I know you?"

"I am Korol, brother to Khall." He paused to let his words take effect.

Images came crashing down on Kirk. Images he had tried to bury years ago, tried and failed. A jungle planet. A fight to the death, man to man. Khall, dreaded, merciless Khall. Two had set down on that steaming pit of a planet, only one had come back. It had been bad, very bad. He could still feel his hands around Khall's throat, Khall's knife in his side. He hadn't wanted to kill the Klingon, but from the first there had been no other choice. It had been necessary, but still he regretted it. It was not something Kirk was proud of.

No, he had not forgotten Khall, nor was he likely to ever completely shake the memory.

Kirk nodded. "Yes, I remember that day."

Korol's eyes grew harder yet. A twitch pulled the corner of his mouth up. The effect was one of deadly, calculated evil.

"I too remember," said Korol. "It is not something a Klingon is likely to forget. You will pay for what you did to my brother."

Kirk's face was emotionless, hard. He knew he faced a dangerous man. If he was half as sly and treacherous as his brother, nothing but trouble lay ahead.

"I paid heavily for that day," he said carefully, slowly. "Your brother was a worthy opponent." The memory was close to the surface now, too close, bathed in the red fog of remembered pain.

"You lived, Kirk. My brother died. *There* is the difference. You will pay for that difference, pay dearly. Not now, maybe not tomorrow, but someday. Someday, when you least expect it, I will kill you. Slowly. Painfully. It will give me great pleasure. I have sworn the oath of blood upon our father's grave."

Kirk flinched in spite of himself. The oath of blood was the most binding obligation a Klingon could make. It meant that before his peers he had sworn to take revenge in kind. It was a vow never taken lightly. Korol had pledged his life to the destruction of Kirk. All else in his life would be secondary to that quest, all else would be dropped when the opportunity arose to fulfill the vow. He had indeed acquired a powerful enemy.

"Look at my face, Kirk. Look at my face long and look at it hard, for it will haunt you always. It will come to you in dreams, in nightmares. You will see it in shadows, in dark places. One day it will be real and you will die. I look forward to that day."

The screen suddenly went blank.

"They're leaving orbit, Captain," said Sulu, his voice rising a little. "They're making a break for it. Should I change our course?"

Kirk clenched his jaws. There was nothing in the universe he would rather do than give chase and force a showdown. A fight would finish it here and now, there would be no faces in the dark, no nightmares. Even as disabled as they were, the *Enterprise,* given a little luck, could blast the other ship apart.

But he had his orders.

"No, Mr. Sulu. Steady as she goes. We have repairs to make, a job to do."

"Aye, sir."

Kirk realized he was still gripping the arms of his chair. The skin on his knuckles was taut, white, drained of blood. Slowly, consciously, he relaxed his grip. Even as he did so, he realized that there was a new fear in him, something he could never totally relax.

"Mr. Spock," he said. "Take the bridge. Go on yellow alert."

"Yes, Captain."

As he rose, Kirk realized he was drenched with sweat. Walking to the door, his legs shook a little, but he held himself straight and it didn't show.

Kirk walked rapidly down the corridor toward Engineering to check with Scotty on the damage. From the amount of smoke in the hall it was likely to be considerable. He was stopped short by Dr. Flagstone, the last person on the ship Kirk wanted to see at that time.

"Captain, I demand to know what is happening."

"You *what?*"

"Why are we being delayed? What did all those sirens mean?"

Kirk took a deep breath to get his temper under control. It would be too easy to step on the old man, a cheap shot. "We have been under attack, Dr. Flagstone.

We will be delayed only as long as it takes to repair the damage, no longer. Then we will be on our way again."

"Those people on Waycross need our supplies and medical team."

"I'm aware of that, Doctor. We are doing all that we can. Now if you would be so kind as—"

"Can I be of any help, Captain?" A young woman approached them. Tall, long dark hair. It was Dr. Kelly Davis, one of the team of specialists that Dr. Flagstone was taking to Waycross.

"Yes, thank you, Dr. Davis," said Kirk. "I was headed back to Engineering. There are injured people. Perhaps Dr. McCoy could use some help."

"Let's go," she said without hesitation, taking his arm.

Dr. Flagstone stood where he was, confused. "Injured people?" he muttered. "You didn't mention—"

"You never gave me a chance," said Kirk, disappearing down the corridor with Dr. Davis.

It looked bad, but not as bad as Kirk had feared. The major damage was confined to the auxiliary machinery room on deck nine and the observation lounge just below it. Kelly Davis wasted no time helping the injured. She was everywhere, doing all she could. Sometimes it just wasn't enough. Three dead, twelve injured, two of them seriously.

Kirk saw Scotty across the smoke-filled room. The burly Scotsman's uniform was torn, his face smudged with soot. In frustration he swung his fist against the wall. Kirk looked away. He understood how Scotty felt.

As they finished the repairs to the *Enterprise,* Captain Kirk had an unpleasant task to fulfill. With a ceremonial crew and three caskets he beamed down to the surface of the unnamed, uncharted planet.

Dust-blown wind whipped around them, got in their eyes, settled in their clothes. The sun overhead was a dull orange globe through the airborne grit. A lousy place to spend eternity. Large stones were gathered, a cairn prepared. Kirk said the words he had said so many times before. He knew them by heart, still they never came easy. Someday, he felt, they would be said for him, probably in a place not too much different than this. Dust gritted in his teeth. *Dust to dust,* he thought. A pile of stones to mark the passing of good men and women. They gave the planet a name. They called it Tombstone. Then they turned their backs on the dead and left. Life was for the living and they had a job to do, lives to live.

"Relax a little, Jim. You couldn't have prevented it. No one could."

Kirk was far from relaxing. He sat on the edge of a diagnostic bed, muscles knotted. Tense.

"I feel like one of those targets at the Academy, Bones. You know, the ones with the large circles painted on them."

"You or the ship, Jim? Which has the circle? Which do you worry for the most?"

Kirk looked up sharply. "Does it make a difference?" he asked. "I'm the target, at least as far as Korol is concerned. They have the ability to sneak up on the ship at any time. They get me, they get the ship." He stared at the floor for a long second.

"You're right, damn it, Bones. You always are. Okay. Let's get it out in the open. I'm worried about me. I'm worried about the ship. I *always* worry about the ship, that's my job, my life. But I'm tired and that worries me, too. I've been stretched pretty thin the last few months, we all have. Things just keep piling up— little things, big things. The ship has been through a lot recently; too much, really. We both, the ship and I, show the strain. I wouldn't tell anyone but you. Of course you knew it already."

"So does Spock, of course."

Kirk nodded silently. Spock wouldn't be First Officer

8

if he didn't notice things like that. He wouldn't be Spock, either.

"The ship I can't prescribe for," said Dr. McCoy, turning, "but for its Captain I have a little medication that just might help." He took out a bottle of five-star Dimian brandy. Aged ten years, the old way. Oak barrels. Good stuff.

"Bones, I—"

"Fifty cc's, Jim, taken orally. Doctor's orders."

"I don't think so."

"You don't have any choice. In matters medical I have the last word." He took two beakers from the cabinet, broke the seal on the bottle. He was starting to pour as the door slid open.

Kelly Davis started to enter the room, stopped, stepped back into the corridor, uncertain as to whether to proceed or not.

"Am I interrupting anything?" she asked.

"Not at all, my dear," said Dr. McCoy, walking to her, taking her arm, guiding her into the room. "I was just prescribing a little medication for the Captain and the ship's Chief Medical Officer. Perhaps you would consider joining us."

Kelly saw the open bottle and grinned. "Maybe just a little," she said.

"Delighted," said Dr. McCoy, taking another beaker down from the cabinet.

"I never got to thank you properly, Dr. Davis."

"For what, Captain?"

"For getting me away from that . . . from Dr. Flagstone. I appreciated that. Also the way you cared for the injured. Thanks for both."

She smiled, accepted the beaker that Dr. McCoy handed her.

"The injured . . ." She stared into the beaker, swirled the amber liquid around. "Well, that's my job. More than that, I guess. I've never been able to stand still when there's something I can do to help, to ease

9

the pain." She took a small sip, made a face and grinned sheepishly. "Strong stuff." She suppressed a cough.

"Dr. Flagstone's okay," she said. "Or he will be when we get to Waycross. He's just puffed up with his own importance. He's really a very good doctor."

"And this is one very good doctor, herself," said McCoy, sitting on the edge of his desk. "A virologist by training, but very good with the nuts and bolts of taking care of sick and injured patients. I'd be pleased to have her at my side anytime. Or be by hers."

"Coming from you, Bones, that's a pretty high recommendation."

"I meant it. Every word of it."

"Come on," said Kelly. "You could charm a bird out of a tree like that."

"If birds came like you, I might try."

Kirk laughed and even as he laughed he wondered if this was also therapy, beautifully designed and executed by the multitalented Dr. McCoy. He decided it didn't matter. He felt a little better. He sipped his drink, wondering how in the blazes Dr. McCoy always seemed to find such good medicine. Smooth, too.

Kelly leaned against McCoy's desk. She seemed relaxed. "How long do you expect it to be, Captain, before we reach Waycross?"

"Almost two days, a little less, probably," said Kirk. "Normally it wouldn't take that long, but our dilithium crystals are in pretty bad shape. We have no choice but to take it easy."

"Then my work will start," she said. "I'll be pretty busy for a while."

"Is it very serious?" asked Kirk.

"Not yet, but it could be. These things have a way of changing overnight."

"What things?"

"We think it's some form of a mutated virus. Probably a local one, but it could have been introduced from someplace else. So far all it's done is make everybody sick, very sick. It's not fatal, at least not yet, but it's bad enough. They've lost ninety percent of their work force. Nearly everyone is bedridden. We've come across this kind of thing before on other planets. Sometimes they mutate quickly after they've adjusted to humans, other times they don't seem to change at all. We can usually work something out, though. We carry a pretty extensive laboratory."

Kirk nodded. He'd seen their equipment when it had been brought aboard. Everything was of the very latest design. McCoy had nosed around it for a long time like a small kid looking over another child's toys. He had been impressed and, Kirk realized, a little envious.

"Sounds like you'll have your hands full," he said.

She smiled and gave an easy laugh. "We usually do. New planets mean new problems, new diseases. The further man pushes, the more complex his problems seem to become."

"I'll go along with that," said Kirk.

"What will you do after you leave us at Waycross, Captain? Where will you go? Off to another new planet with new problems?"

Kirk laughed. "No, not this time. Nothing as exciting as that. We'll be heading directly back to Starbase 6. The ship and crew could use a little patching up, a little rest. The dilithium crystals aren't the only things around here that need attention."

"Including the Captain," added McCoy.

Kirk nodded. That much was true.

Forty-six hours later, the *Enterprise* hung in orbit above the planet Waycross. It had been an uneventful two days. Uneventful, that is, except for the strain—the strain of expecting the Klingon ship to appear at any moment, the strain of nursing the *Enterprise* along at half power, the strain of the past few months building among the ship's crew and officers—months of long periods of inactivity and boredom followed by split-second decisions, frantic activity, and the unleashing of vast amounts of awesome power. All this had taken its toll on the ship and crew. Most of them couldn't wait to beam down the doctors and supplies so they could head for Starbase 6 and their much-deserved rest.

Captain Kirk settled into his chair on the bridge. The unloading was routine. "Ensign Chekov, go down to the transporter room and give Scotty a hand."

The young man jumped to his feet. "Yes, sir," he said and was gone. He was always anxious to please, sometimes too anxious. Eventually he would make a top officer, Kirk was sure about that, but for now he had a few rough edges that needed rounding off.

Kirk looked down at the green globe that was Way-cross. Someday, perhaps, it would be a great agricultural planet. It had a good, rich soil and a multitude of plants grew well there. As yet there was just a small colony on the planet, but more would come and the population would grow. In a way the planet symbolized man's reach for the stars. It had been hard at first, very hard, but mankind was an animal that didn't give up easily. The rewards were slow in coming, but rich indeed. Now man lived on a variety of planets scattered throughout the universe. It had been a struggle, but the results were well worth it. He wondered what it must have been like when all of humanity lived on a single planet, with only one planet's resources. Grimly, he shook his head. He knew the facts, some of them. Mankind had come close to poisoning the only home they had. For a while in the twentieth century, they had to live with the very real possibility that war could wipe out the entire human race. Now, scattered as they were, it would be nearly impossible. They also treated the planets they lived on more gently now, with greater respect.

We have learned that much, he thought.

In the subdued lighting of the corridor outside Transporter Room Three, a shimmer of light was briefly visible as a figure materialized. The man ducked into the shadows and quietly worked his way to the entrance. He pressed against the wall for a moment, and when he judged the time was right, he slipped inside.

There were four people in the room, their backs to him, huddled around a pile of equipment on the auxiliary transporter platform. He made no noise. Dropping to his knees, he attached a small device to the underside of the controls to the transporter. Quickly, he connected a few wires, pushed them out of sight. He rose silently and went to the door, placing a small package off to one side of the room where he was sure it would be found later. Seeing the corridor was clear, he stepped out into it, whispered into a communicator and vanished in a rain of sparkles.

Satisfied that everything was in order, Ensign Chekov slid the transporter controls into position. The room was filled with a blinding flash of light.

It was the last thing he remembered.

Kirk arrived at the scene just seconds after the emergency crew. Debris was everywhere, the room was filled with a thick, black smoke.

"What happened?" he asked. "Scotty—*what happened?*"

"I dinna' know, Captain. I was busy and sent Chekov here to—"

"Chekov. Is he—"

"No, he's okay, sir. As well as can be expected, considerin' the circumstances. They were transportin' the last o' the lab equipment doon from here. Most o' the doctors had already left from the main transporter room. The equipment was bein' sent from here. It must ha'e been a malfunction. Everythin' blew on the platform."

"At least it was only equipment," said Kirk.

"I'm afraid not," said Scotty. "One of the doctors was stayin' behind to help load the equipment. A lady doctor."

"Dr. Davis?"

"Aye, that's the one. She's in verra bad shape. Dr. McCoy is with her now."

Kirk shook his head. Kelly. Damn, what next? If anyone could save her life, Bones could.

A security guard approached the two men. He held a small package.

"Excuse me, Captain," he said. "I found this over by the door. It's a—"

"I know what it is," snapped Kirk, taking it in his hand. "Find out what happened."

"Yes, sir," he said, backing off.

Kirk turned it over in his hands. A tape cassette, Klingon origin. What was it doing here?

"Let me know as soon as you find anything," he said to Scotty. "I'll be on the Bridge."

"Aye, sir," he said, watching the Captain storm out the door.

Lieutenant Uhura was startled when Kirk burst onto the bridge. There was a wild look in his eyes, a mixture of pain and rage. He smelled of smoke, there were black smudges on his face and clothes. He appeared to be holding a great deal inside of him, barely under the surface, barely under control. He practically threw the tape cassette at her.

"Put this on the screen. Now." He turned abruptly and went to his chair.

"Yes, *sir*," she mumbled under her breath, working the tape into the slot.

The face that appeared on the screen was familiar this time, all too familiar. Korol looked down at the crew on the bridge; his face larger than life, contorted by a twisted, sardonic smile.

"That could have been you, Kirk," the taped image said. "It could have easily been you. But that would have been a cheap way out—too easy, too quick. That would have been a simple killing, not revenge. I want you to suffer, suffer as my brother did. At night I trust you will see the faces of those I hope died in your place. Knowing you as I do, I am sure it will give you great anguish. Humanitarianism is one of your weak spots, Kirk, and I intend to use it. I will do everything I can to make your remaining days unbearable, your remaining nights filled with demons. *Then* I will kill you. Sleep well, Kirk. Sleep well."

The screen went blank. The Bridge was silent, hushed.

"That's all, sir," said Uhura quietly.

Kirk shook his head. No, that wasn't all. Not by a long shot.

CHAPTER TWO

Captain's Log, Stardate 6831.4:

We are leaving the planet Waycross with our course
set for Starbase 6. The crew has been scheduled for
R&R while the ship undergoes repairs and the
dilithium crystals are replenished. The entire sensor network of the ship will be dismantled and
checked. Star Fleet Command is as confused about
this as we are. There are no indications whatsoever
as to how the Klingon ship got close enough to
transport a man or team of men aboard to rig the
transporter board without being detected. It is
hoped that an examination of the ship might pro-
vide some information, but that seems doubtful.
Our own crews, despite several exhaustive searches,
have turned up nothing.

Mention was made to Star Fleet Command of the
blood oath sworn on me by the Klingon Korol, but
that has rightly been assumed to be incidental to
the immediate problem.

The U.S.S. *Phoenix* will be bringing replacement
equipment and an additional doctor to Waycross.

Due to the extent of her injuries and the medical
facilities available, Dr. Kelly Davis will remain on
board the *Enterprise*. Her condition is stable.

In the muted lights of sick bay, Dr. McCoy passed
the remote sensor over the still form of Kelly Davis.

Her breathing was ragged, an uneven gasping in the quiet room. The readouts on the graphic display above the diagnostic bed were low, but satisfactory under the circumstances. It looked better than he had expected. Kelly Davis was a strong woman.

McCoy straightened up, rubbed his stiff back. It had been close for a while, he'd almost lost her. She would need lots of rest, but it looked like she was going to pull through. Now she slept, a deep sleep.

Nurse Christine Chapel entered the darkened room, walked over to McCoy. "Excuse me, Doctor," she said, touching his sleeve. "I've finished with Ensign Chekov. He and the Captain are waiting in your office."

McCoy turned away from the bed, nodded. "Keep an eye on her, Nurse. If she starts to come around, give her a sedative. She needs the rest."

Drawing up a chair, Nurse Chapel sat down beside the bed as Dr. McCoy left the room.

"How about it Doc?" asked Chekov in an anxious voice. "Am I going to make it?" His hands and face were covered with a light salve. Kirk stood next to him, leaning against McCoy's desk.

"I guess so," said McCoy. "You're tough. Must be all that Russian blood in you."

"I still feel a little shaky," he said. "Can I go?"

McCoy nodded. "Get some rest, though. Stay in your quarters for a day or two. As soon as your hands heal you can go back to work. Take it easy until then, though. Give that salve a chance to work."

Chekov left, the door giving a faint hiss as it slid closed behind him. McCoy turned to face Kirk.

"Just a few flash burns, Jim. Nothing much to worry about. Nothing, that is, from the accident."

Kirk looked at McCoy sharply. "What do you mean by that?"

"I talked to him about the accident. There was a split second after he'd moved the transporter controls before the blast. He felt something was wrong and

17

tried to shut down the board. He couldn't do it quickly enough." McCoy was silent for a second. "He blames himself, Jim, and in a way he's right."

"That's just not possible."

"I'm afraid it is. He should have been able to react fast enough to shut down the board. He had just enough time to do it, but he wasn't quick enough. I gave him a thorough examination. His reflexes are slow, too slow. Suboptimal values almost all the way across. Nothing serious taken individually, but added together they mean trouble."

"What kind of trouble, Bones?"

"Without getting technical about it, let me just say that he's generally weak and rundown. I think this tour is finally catching up with him. It's been a strain, Jim, more than you probably realize."

"I could take Chekov off duty for a while. We'll be arriving at Starbase 6 soon."

"It's not just Chekov, I'm afraid. The problem's much bigger than that. I picked out ten of the crew at random and checked them. They all showed essentially the same results as Chekov. I have a strong feeling I could check a hundred without seeing anything different. The crew needs shore leave badly."

"That's what we're headed for."

McCoy shook his head. "Not good enough, Jim, not soon enough. If their work was less critical it probably wouldn't be important, but this is a starship—*a starship*. At any time the crew could be called on to perform like the superhumans everyone thinks they ought to be. They just won't be able to do it. Mentally and physically, they're way below par. I suggest you enforce an accelerated program of exercise and drill until we reach Starbase 6."

"I suppose you're right, Bones. They won't like it, but—"

"Bridge to Captain," crackled Uhura's voice over the intercom.

Kirk leaned across the desk to McCoy's unit, thumbed the button. "Kirk here."

"Captain, you're wanted on the bridge. We have an incoming call from the U.S.S. *Phoenix*. A Vice-Commodore Propp requests to speak with you."

"On my way," he said. "Kirk out."

Sighing, Kirk headed for the door. Propp was with Star Fleet Command. "I wonder what they want this time?" he muttered.

Lieutenant Uhura put the call through as soon as Kirk reached the bridge. He found himself facing the image of a man only slightly older than himself, a man who had gone through the ranks quickly. He was lightly bearded, heavyset, looked like he was much more comfortable in deep space than behind a desk. He nodded at Kirk.

"It's been a long time, Jim," he said.

"True enough, Larry. Too long." Propp had served with Kirk several years ago. They'd had some good times together, been through some rough ones. "What brings you to this corner of the Galaxy?"

"I got all tangled up in this Waycross business. You know me: Star Fleet Command's chief flunky. If something goes wrong, just send old Larry out to fix it. I'll probably be stuck on Waycross for a month."

"Sounds like the old days," said Kirk with a smile.

"It is, just about." He paused, looked around.

"This isn't just a social call, is it, Larry?" asked Kirk.

"No, Jim. I'm afraid not. I've been in contact with Fleet Headquarters, and they wanted me to relay a message to you. It concerns a planet called Perry."

"Perry? I'm not familiar with that planet."

"Wouldn't expect you to be. We don't know much about it either, no more than you have in your computer. It was the destination of a group of colonists that left Earth some three hundred years ago. The records back that far aren't too clear. It seems they used a modified ramjet, ion-drive ship, something ar-

19

chaic like that. Nothing was ever heard from them after they left the solar system. It was naturally assumed that the mission had failed. Many did, back in those days."

"I know that, Larry. But what does that have to do with us? We're headed for Starbase 6."

"Not any more. I'm sorry Jim, orders from the top. You're headed for Perry, now."

"*Larry!* We're way overdue for repairs. My crew needs a rest badly. This mission has already been extended three times. Star Fleet wants to examine our sensors. What's so important about Perry?"

"To begin with, it's inhabited. Star Fleet Command received a one-way subspace transmission from them. Evidently the colonists made it. Someone has to go."

"Why us?"

"First, you're the closest available ship of the *constitution* class to the planet. Second, you're the most qualified person we have in the field right now to undertake this particular type of mission."

"*What* type of mission?" asked Kirk suspiciously.

"Diplomatic."

"You've got to be kidding."

"Sorry, no. The communication we received requested that the United Federation of Planets send a representative to discuss the possibilities of Perry joining the Federation. That's all they said. You're the best man we have for this and the closest. It can't go any other way. It's important, Jim, or we wouldn't have you do it."

"I know," said Kirk, shaking his head. "I know. It's a bad time for it, that's all."

"Everyone's aware of the condition of your ship. The decision was reached that the circumstances warranted a slight delay. It shouldn't take long."

"I hope so, Larry. I sincerely hope so."

As he broke the connection, Kirk thought of other diplomatic missions he'd undertaken. Some went smoothly, some didn't. They all took time. He hoped this would be one of the smooth ones. He swiveled his chair to the right.

"Mr. Spock," he said. "What information do we have on the planet?"

"Not much more than the vice-commodore indicated, Captain. The planet he was referring to is a class M one, the fourth planet out in a system of eight around that particular star. Since it is located in a fairly remote corner of the Galaxy, it has never been surveyed. The U.S.S. *Potemkin* was scheduled to make a routine investigation of that sector in six months. It appears that the investigation will no longer be necessary."

"Any information in the computer on the colonists, Mr. Spock?"

"Very little. It was a fairly large group, selected from volunteers. There were no religious or political beliefs held in common as far as we know. Evidently they used a modified form of suspended animation, a freeze-sleep technique that would have taken two generations to reach the planet. Their leader was a man called Wayne Perry, a philanthropist of great wealth at the time. Apparently he had some sort of a scientific background, though the computer has no specific information on this point. The planet seems to have been named in his memory. According to their original estimates, they should have reached the planet some two hundred and fifty years ago if everything had gone according to plan. There is no indication, of course, that it did."

Kirk nodded, well aware that there had been many failures among mankind's early attempts at space exploration, especially with the colonies. A very high percentage of the expeditions never succeeded. Of those that did, many fell victim to their own planet, others reverted to barbarism or worse. Out of the mainstream of civilization, many of the cultures had evolved in strange ways. The results were varied, and often unpleasant. This one, at least, seemed to know of the presence of the United Federation of Planets and had achieved a level of technology capable of interstellar communication, even if it was primitive, one-way subspace transmission. It could be worse. Maybe this *would* be one of the smooth ones. Maybe it would go quickly.

He had his hopes, but he had his doubts, too. Things were rarely what they seemed to be on the surface.

CHAPTER THREE

Captain's Log, Stardate 6834.5.:

We are in orbit around the planet Perry, preparing to embark on the assigned diplomatic mission. The planet seems remarkably suitable to human life. Apparently there is but one large city, although there are many cultivated farms and small villages scattered throughout the three major land masses. The polar areas are small, there are few deserts. Most of the land is green and lightly wooded. It is not, by appearance, a harsh planet. Perhaps the colonists had an easy time of it.

Accompanying me to the planet's surface will be First Officer Spock and Chief Medical Officer Leonard McCoy. Our assignment is to convince the ruling body of this planet of the advantages in joining the United Federation of Planets. It is hoped that this assignment can be accomplished in a short period of time, as we are anxious to continue on to Starbase 6.

Doctor Kelly Davis continues to recover. Her determination to return to normal activities is matched only by the extraordinary medical skills exhibited by Dr. McCoy in her behalf. Today she walked unaided for the first time since the incident.

"Do I really have to go through with this, Jim?" asked McCoy, standing in the transporter room, tugging at his full-dress uniform.

"As a ranking officer, Bones, you should be along for the negotiations. Besides, I think you cut a dashing figure all dessed up like that. It ought to help our image."

"Image be damned," grumbled McCoy. "This confounded uniform is too blasted tight. If I didn't know better, I'd swear it had shrunk."

"It's not possible that you're putting on a little weight, is it?"

"Not a chance, Jim. I haven't put on an ounce in years."

Kirk looked at McCoy questioningly, doubtfully.

"Well, not *that* much, anyway," said McCoy.

Kirk laughed softly, well aware that more than the uniform was bothering the doctor. McCoy's reluctance to use the transporter was common knowledge among the crew and often the subject of mild-mannered kidding and joking. But the memory of the incident in Transporter Room Three was all too fresh in their minds. There would be no kidding about that today. But that didn't mean that Kirk couldn't try to get McCoy's mind off the subject.

"It'll be good for you," said Kirk. "You might even enjoy this mission. Perhaps under that crusty exterior you have the makings of a real diplomat."

"Thanks, Jim," said McCoy dryly. "I'd rather dig ditches. At least that's honest work."

"Come on, Bones. Relax a little. Let someone else take care of the crabby crew members and ingrown toenails for a while."

McCoy shot Kirk a glance that seemed to indicate that he thought the Captain was the crabbiest of all the crew members. At least he wasn't worrying about the transporter.

Spock entered the room with a tricorder slung over one shoulder. "Everything is in order, Captain," he said. "I have confirmed our appointment with their Council. We will be met upon arrival."

"Very good, Mr. Spock." Kirk paused, gave the transporter platform a quick, uneasy look, stepped up onto it. Spock and McCoy followed him.

"Might as well get this show on the road," he said. "Take good care of the ship, Mr. Scott."

"Aye, sir. I'll do just that."

"Places."

Kirk had a vague feeling of uncomfortableness, which he tried to bury. Everything had been thoroughly checked out. He wondered what McCoy must be feeling.

"Energize."

In the sparkle of three glittering columns the men materialized in the middle of a broad, cobblestone square. Two of the men wore expressions of immense relief. The third was stony-faced and calm as ever. Nothing ever seemed to bother Spock. He unstrapped the tricorder and took some preliminary readings. Kirk and McCoy caught the relief in each other's faces and broke into silly, sheepish grins.

The buildings surrounding the square were short, solid, and obviously well-built. The liberal use of stone and rough wood in their construction seemed to be an indication of a rustic background, while the presence of plastic and more modern materials indicated an advanced technology of some sort. It would take a while to gather impressions, sort everything out. It was cool, the air was fresh and clean.

The arrival of the three men hadn't caused much of a stir. Although the square and surrounding area wasn't exactly crowded, it wasn't deserted either. Strangely enough, nobody seemed to pay much attention to their unorthodox method of appearing. They weren't exactly ignored, either. People passing by them would smile, or nod politely, and pass on; always without speaking. They were all dressed alike, men and women, children and adults: in slacks with loose shirts, all a similar shade of dark brown. The only bright colors in evidence were scarves worn by the adults, loosely tied around their necks. Just as Kirk was turning to Spock, a young man and woman started to approach them. Kirk noticed they wore yellow scarves. Perhaps a badge of office. He stepped forward to meet them.

"I am Captain James T. Kirk of the Starship *Enterprise,*" he said. "We are here as representatives of the United Federation of Planets."

The girl laughed easily, a light, gentle laugh, like the tinkling of a far-off bell. "No need to be so formal, Captain. We've been expecting you. I'm called Ami and this is Rus. We are pages at the Council. If it pleases you, we will escort you and your men to the Council chambers."

Kirk relaxed a little, almost smiled. "It pleases us," he said. "Lead on."

They left the square by a narrow street that wound among the low buildings. Evidently a mixture of residential houses and small businesses, few of the buildings were more than two stories high. Most had a balcony along the second floor, where people sat or stood quietly. An ivy-like plant covered many of the buildings and balconies. A small vehicle hummed slowly down the middle of the street.

"Propulsion, Mr. Spock?" asked Kirk, indicating the machine.

"Solar powered, Captain. It apparently utilizes a rather large storage battery, judging from its shape. I would suspect it has serious limitations in both range and speed. Quite primitive."

Kirk nodded, taking in as many details as possible. He was sure Spock was doing the same. It was habit. It was necessary. On a new planet, no matter how calm the outward signs, it was vital to collect as much information as possible as soon as possible. Kirk didn't like surprises.

26

Although there were many people walking along the sidewalk, it never seemed crowded. They gave way to each other with polite smiles and small bows. The reactions they gave to Kirk and his men were no different than they gave anyone else. There were no signs of the hurried jostling and short tempers that Kirk had found so common in other large cities. It was a pleasant change from the minor bickering and tense atmosphere that had developed in the ship recently.

"Tell me, Ami," asked Kirk, "is it always so quiet here?"

She looked puzzled. "Quiet?" she said. "I can hear many noises. The mobiles hum in the streets and the people talk and laugh as they go their ways. There are noises, many of them."

"What I mean," explained Kirk, "is that everybody seems so calm and unconcerned. Nobody seemed to notice us arrive or be in the least concerned about us walking among them."

"They know that you are different," said Rus. "You dress strangely and one of you is obviously an alien of some sort. You wear the mark of no guild. But of what matter is that? You have business here or you wouldn't be among us. If it concerns the people they will be told about it. It is not polite to pry into someone else's business, and we are a polite people. What does not concern them does not bother them."

"It's simply common courtesy," added Ami. "We live and let live here on Perry. It makes it much easier to get along."

"It sounds good in theory," said McCoy, "but I've never seen it work in practice, especially with large groups. There are always malcontents, troublemakers."

"There are no troublemakers on Perry," said Rus in a firm voice, drawing the words out slowly. "None at all."

As they continued down the sidewalk, McCoy wondered what Rus meant by that. So did Kirk.

Spock was busy taking unobtrusive tricorder readings as they walked. He had found some interesting pieces of data. Very interesting.

It wasn't far to the Council Chambers, a small, nondescript building not much different from any of the surrounding ones. A small brass plaque on the wall was the only thing that set it apart. As they approached the door, Rus held it open but Spock stepped back, touched Kirk's shoulder.

"Captain," he whispered. "This building is evidently heavily shielded. The tricorder is unable to penetrate it."

Kirk nodded and they entered.

It was cool inside, high ceilings, heavily paneled walls, a few portraits. They were led down a long hall to a rather large but unpretentious room. Two men and two women sat around a long table. There were several empty chairs. They rose as Kirk and his men entered.

Ami made the introduction of the *Enterprise* crew to the Council members. The two men were called Jon and Mika, the women were Dawn and Joan. No last names were given and there was an air of easy familiarity among the group, a distinct lack of any noticeable protocol. The Council members were dressed identically as Rus and Ami, with the exception of their scarves, which were gold.

"Make yourselves at home. Please have a seat," said the one called Jon, who, by appearances was the eldest of the group. He indicated a grouping of overstuffed chairs with a casual swing of his arm. "Ami, would you please do us the favor of providing refreshments?"

Ami nodded and left the room as the men sat down. The Council members drew up chairs and sat among them. Kirk was anxious to get down to business, but there were formalities to things like this, rituals to perform, even when you weren't too sure what the rituals were. It was better to play things by ear, not to rush anything. The chairs were comfortable.

Kirk turned to Jon, who appeared to be the person in charge. "You seem to have adjusted well to this planet," he said.

Jon smiled, nodded. "It was not easy at first, but not nearly so difficult as had been anticipated. This planet has been kind to us. We, in turn, are kind to it. It provides us with what we need."

Spock spoke up. "It would seem that this planet is a particularly suitable one for human life."

"Yes," answered Jon. "It was our ancestor's first choice. When they arrived, the colony began immediately. They worked hard. We have all worked hard." He paused, looked up as Ami entered the room with a tray ringed with small glasses, piled high in the middle with delicate pastries. "Ah, refreshments," he said.

Ami stopped in front of Kirk. He took one of the glasses and a pastry, although he wasn't hungry or thirsty. He waited until everyone was served and stood to offer a toast.

"Ladies and gentlemen," he said, raising his glass. "To peace across the universe."

Jon smiled broadly. "Yes indeed," he said. "Peace by all means. Peace by *any* means."

Kirk tipped his glass in reply, drained it as they did. It was warm and sticky, didn't seem alcoholic at all. He sat down, turned to Jon.

"You sent for us," said Kirk. "Therefore you must have some knowledge of the United Federation of Planets and the advantages to aligning yourselves with us."

Jon nodded. "We do have some limited technology. Not that we're backward, by any means, but we're not nearly as advanced as you. While your technology has been advancing, we have been busy colonizing this planet. We made advances, to be sure, but they are along other lines. For a long time we have been able to monitor your communications, but until recently we have lacked the ability to respond. The Blues can tell you more about that later, it really isn't within my field."

"Blues?" asked Kirk.

"Technos? Technocrats? I'm not sure of your word for them. They handle our physical sciences. I will introduce you to some later, if you wish. Anyone with a blue scarf can tell you more than I would be able to."

"The scarves indicate occupation?" asked Kirk.

"We have a guild system here. Young people apprentice themselves at an early age to a guild that fits their aptitudes. The are assigned a Master to learn from and are given a sash or scarf of the appropriate color. All apprentices start out initially wearing pastel hues of their color. As they increase in knowledge they receive belts of increasingly brighter shades. Thus, a blue sash is a techno, but the degree of brightness is indicative of their level within the field."

"I've seen similar systems before," said Kirk.

"I can't speak for the others," said Jon, "but it works well for us."

"I'm sure your technology could benefit greatly from association with the Federation," said Kirk, setting his empty glass on a tray passed by Ami.

"Possibly," said Jon. "I'm sure that there are advantages and disadvantages to joining, as there are in any relationship. But that decision does not rest with us."

"No?" asked Kirk, surprised.

"The Council is concerned more in the day-to-day affairs of the planet. A long-reaching decision of this sort would have to be the will of the people, with, of course, ultimate responsibility resting on Captain Perry."

"Captain Wayne Perry?" asked Kirk incredulously. That was simply not possible.

"Of course," said Jon. "He is the protective and

30

benevolent ruler of our planet. He brought us here from the stars. All major decisions are referred to him. He should be along shortly. Currently he is meditating."

Kirk looked at Spock in amazement. Wayne Perry had been the captain of the colonists' ship. If this was true, he would be over *three hundred* years old!

"We look forward to meeting Captain Perry," said Spock. It was a typical Vulcan understatement.

31

CHAPTER FOUR

Chief Engineer Scott stood in the corridor. He wasn't happy. He had his hands full. One hand held an angry crewman with a rapidly swelling black eye, the other, an equally angry crewman with a bloody nose.

"I dinna' suppose either of you want to tell me how this happened?" he said.

The two men glared at each other. Scotty gave them a little shake for good measure.

"You, *Mister* Shaw," he said, letting loose of one of the men. "And how did you get such a beautiful shiner?'"

"I beg your pardon, sir?" he said, touching the side of his face gingerly.

"You understan' whit I'm talkin' aboot. That marvelous puffy eye."

"Oh that, sir," he said hesitantly. "I'm afraid I tripped, sir. Fell down."

Scotty turned his attention to the other man. "And you, Mister Kukar? That's a mighty bent nose you got there."

Kukar looked down, stared at the floor. "Same thing, sir," he mumbled. "I fell down." He was clenching and unclenching his fists.

"Ah," said Scotty. "That explains it. Whit we have here is an epidemic of fallin' doon goin' around the ship. I should have known. Treacherous things, these floors, sneak up an' get you if you don't pay attention.

32

Suppose we all take a walk doon to sick bay and see if we can get this thing taken care of."

Scotty held them until they were more or less steady on their feet, pointed them in the direction of sick bay.

Shaw spoke up, quietly. "Sir, may I ask if this will go on our records? In our permanent file?"

Scotty managed the barest of smiles. "For fallin' doon? I seriously doubt it." His face became stern again. "Of course, if it was somehow to happen again, it might not sit too well with me. Do we understan' each other?"

Shaw nodded. "Thank you, sir. It won't happen again, I assure you."

"I'm sure it won't," said Scotty, but he wasn't sure at all.

When they reached sick bay, Nurse Chapel hardly looked up. "What do you have this time, Mr. Scott? Did these men walk into another wall?"

"No. Believe it or no', these two tripped and fell. Seems to be a lot of it goin' around."

"Their injuries appear to be quite minor," she said. "But I'm sure that if I look around hard enough, I can find a painful and uncomfortable cure."

"No doubt you can," said Scotty. "Thank you verra much."

Stepping out into the hall as he was leaving sick bay, Scotty nearly bumped into Kelly Davis passing by.

"Excuse me, Dr. Davis," he said, aware that she was still recuperating. "I hope I didn't—I mean, I wasn't watchin' where I was goin'."

She laughed. "It's all right, Mr. Scott. I'm not made of glass, you know."

"Sorry," said Scotty, embarrassed. "It's just, well . . ."

"I know," said Kelly with a smile. "You all think

I ought to be pampered. You forget I've knocked around on some pretty rough planets. Dr. McCoy advised as much exercise as I can tolerate. Walking is good exercise, so I've been walking all over the ship. Would you care to join me for a while?"

"I was headin' back to Engineerin'," he said.

"Then I'll go that way."

"Fair enough," he said, and they started down the corridor. He had to resist the temptation to take her arm. She was still a bit unsteady, despite what she said.

After they had gone a short distance, Kelly spoke up. "They were having a fight, weren't they?"

"Who?" asked Scotty. "What do you mean?"

"Those two men you brought to sick bay. I saw them. They looked like they'd been in a fight."

"Well, it mighta been a minor altercation, but I wouldna' call it a fight," said Scotty. "Nothin' serious."

Kelly nodded. "I've seen it before."

"What's that?"

"Cabin fever," she said. "I guess the worst I've ever seen was on Palvin, a planet they once shipped me to. It was cold there, everything stayed frozen over for more than ninety percent of the year. Nobody could go anywhere, they all had to stay in small, depressing shacks staring at the same faces day after day. By the time the thaw came, they were at each other's throats constantly."

"Beggin' yer pardon, Miss Davis, but I don't think that could happen on the *Enterprise*."

"It may already be happening, Mr. Scott."

"The men will be fine once we get to Starbase 6, I'm sure of that."

"I don't doubt that, but—"

She was cut off by the intercom. "Bridge to Mr. Scott," came Uhura's voice. It sounded urgent.

Scott stepped over and punched the nearest unit on the wall. "Scott here," he said.

"Mr. Scott, we have lost contact with the Captain."

"Lost contact? How?"

"There are several locations on the planet that our sensors cannot probe. Evidently they have entered one of those areas."

"I'm on my way," he said, turning toward the Bridge, leaving Kelly Davis standing alone.

Nothing seemed to be going right.

Captain Kirk didn't like the way the situation was developing. On a new planet he liked to have all the facts fit neatly together, but no matter how hard he tried he couldn't fit this new twist into it at all. Wayne Perry couldn't be the same person who captained the the original ship. He couldn't be three hundred years old. Yet it seemed like the Council members believed it. He could only assume the rest of the inhabitants of the planet felt the same way. It didn't make any sense at all.

At any rate, one thing that Kirk had learned in his years of command was to roll with the punches, expect the unexpected. To his credit, his composure didn't slip a notch as a side door slid open and a man apparently in his mid-thirties appeared. Sandy hair, just a touch of gray, he looked younger than the Council members. Everybody rose. It had to be Wayne Perry, whoever he was. He looked friendly, alert, dignified. He looked anything but three hundred years old.

"Gentlemen," he said to the *Enterprise* crew, "please be seated. I must apologize for not meeting you when you arrived, but I was otherwise occupied." He flashed an engaging smile. "You must be Captain Kirk."

"Yes," nodded Kirk. "And I'd like to present my First Officer Spock and Chief Medical Officer Dr. Leonard McCoy."

"Pleased to meet you. Captain Wayne Perry at your disposal. I suppose you come equipped with a lengthy and informative sales pitch for the United Federation of Planets."

Kirk smiled. "I'd hardly call it a sales pitch. We're not trying to sell you anything, just to outline the advantages of aligning yourselves with the Federation."

Perry leaned back in his chair. "We've been aware of the Federation for quite some time, but until recently we have lacked the ability to communicate with you. Or the desire, for that matter. Your presence in the Galaxy was an interesting, if somewhat abstract fact to us. We have been much too busy on this planet to worry about the affairs of other civilizations. Now this is changing."

"Oh?" said Kirk. "In what way?"

"Our people are showing a renewed interest in space travel. We lack the facilities to achieve that. They also feel, and I agree, that interaction with other people, other civilizations, would keep us from becoming too fixed in our ideas. We do not wish to stagnate as a colony, we wish to grow. Input from other sources would be of great benefit to us at this time. I'm sure that we, in turn, have things to offer the Federation. It could be mutually beneficial."

"I'm sure it would be," said Kirk, who was sure of no such thing. So far all he had seen was a fairly pleasant planet, somewhat backward in technological achievements. If they had anything to offer other than being a nice place to visit, he hadn't seen it yet.

"Suppose I give you a little background on the Federation," he said.

"Please do," said Perry.

"Basically the United Federation of Planets is a democratic political entity, lending support and information to its member planets. We cover numerous star systems including many planets such as Earth and Vulcan, Mr. Spock's home planet. The Federation maintains a considerable variety of services that the

36

planets may draw upon. For example, we have highly advanced medical facilities connected to computers that hold an immense amount of information. The technology of many different races would be available to you. Upon joining the Federation you would send representatives to the Federation Council, and thereby have a voice in its policy. In addition, you would come under the protection of Federation law."

"That last sounds a little unnecessary," said Perry. "We have no crime on this planet."

Kirk doubted that, but decided not to press the matter. "I *have* noticed that things seem very relaxed here."

"We pride ourselves on having developed a peaceful way of life. Perhaps that is what we have to export."

"Peace is a commodity that's always in demand," said Kirk. "Unfortunately the supply is often short."

"I assure you that is not the case here. We do not believe in violence."

"An admirable policy," said Kirk. "But not always practical."

"It could be," said Perry. "Given the right conditions, it could be."

"Even under the ideal conditions, people would still be human," said Kirk. "We would still need laws and regulations." He opened a folder he had brought down from the ship. "I have here a copy of the Articles of Confederation, along with a synopsis of how they would apply to your planet." He stood up, set the papers on the table in front of Perry, who looked down at them with detached interest.

"Abstract these Jon, if you will. Prepare a public referendum on the subject." He turned to Kirk. "I am inclined to accept the offer to join the Federation, or at the very least remain neutral. But I must first put it before the people."

"May I ask how long it will take?" asked Kirk.

"No more than two or three days," said Perry. "These referendums seldom take very long. There are voting stations throughout the city, and others in the remote villages. As soon as Jon prepares the synopsis it will be presented for consideration. This is normal procedure for any such decision. We have no regularly scheduled elections, things are voted on as they come up. In the meantime, I would consider you and your crew our guests here on Perry, and would urge you to avail yourselves of whatever we may offer you."

McCoy leaned over to Kirk. "Shore leave wouldn't be a bad idea, Jim. This looks like a nice enough planet, and I needn't remind you that the crew badly needs a rest."

Kirk nodded. He didn't have to be reminded. "Spock?" he said. "Any objections?"

"None that would preclude shore leave, Captain."

"Then it's settled?" asked Perry.

"Yes," said Kirk. "We'll stay until the question has been decided. Thank you for your generous offer of hospitality, we accept it."

"Good," said Perry, rising. "Now, if you'll excuse me, I have other things to attend to. It has been a genuine pleasure talking with you."

"The pleasure has been mine," said Kirk as Perry left by the same door he had entered by.

Jon gathered the papers from the table. "I'll have the referendum posted this afternoon," he said. "In the meantime, please make yourselves at home. We use no currency in the city, since we operate on a work-exchange basis. As guests, of course, you and your crew are exempt from our exchange system, so please feel free to utilize any of our city's facilities. I particularly recommend the restaurants and pubs around the square. The food and drink are quite acceptable and the company congenial."

"Thank you," said Kirk, rising. Ami escorted them to the door.

"Perhaps you would join us for dinner tonight?" asked Kirk.

Ami nodded. "I'd be delighted," she said. Then she closed the door and the three men stood on the street.

"Well, gentlemen?" asked Kirk, "Opinions?"

"Not an opinion, Captain," said Spock. "But I do have a fact."

"Yes, Mr. Spock?"

"Wayne Perry is not a human being. Furthermore, he isn't even alive."

"*What?*"

"I scanned him with the tricorder as soon as he entered. He is a very sophisticated computer construct —an advanced hologram, if you would prefer to call it that. He is three dimensional and as solid as you or I. But he's no more alive than the sidewalk we are standing on."

"Why didn't you tell me right away?" asked Kirk.

"First, there was no opportunity. Second, in light of our mission, it makes no difference whether we negotiate with a human being or a computer as long as whatever we are dealing with has the power to make decisions on this planet. Third, this fact, while interesting, has no bearing on whether or not the crew should take shore leave, which was the only direct question you asked me."

"Enough," said Kirk. "I suppose you have other reasons."

"Seven major ones, ten minor ones, with endless permutations and subcategories to follow."

"Bones, what do you think about this?"

"I think I'll leave Wayne Perry, whoever or whatever he is, to you two experts. My only concern is that if the crew doesn't get off the ship soon, they're going to pop their corks."

"Their what?" asked Spock.

"Never mind," said McCoy. "You wouldn't understand. Vulcans don't have corks."

Kirk flipped open his communicator. "Kirk to *Enterprise*," he said. "Prepare to beam up the landing party."

And in doing so, he sealed the fate of everyone aboard the starship.

CHAPTER FIVE

Captain's Log, Stardate 6835.1:

We are commencing shore leave on the planet Perry
while awaiting the results of a public referendum
concerning their joining the United Federation of
Planets. The first shift beamed down to the surface
two hours ago and there have been no adverse
signs. The planet seems pleasant enough and the
people are friendly. There remain, however, two
disturbing elements. One is the computer construct
called Wayne Perry, and the other is a heavily
shielded area underneath the city.

Wayne Perry is an enigma. Although reviewing
Spock's tricorder tapes clearly shows that he is not
human, it does not answer any questions as to why
this computer construct exists, or what function it
serves in this society. As far as we can tell, the
residents of the planet are aware that he is "different," but do not think this is at all unusual or worthy
of comment. We plan to explore this at greater
length with the woman known as Ami.

The heavily shielded area beneath the city was
also discovered by Mr. Spock. It can be penetrated
only slightly by the tricorder. Initial analysis indi-
cates diffuse computer activity and some life activity, presumably human. The Council Chambers
appear to be the only building so shielded. Mister

Scott was greatly concerned about loss of contact with us. And rightly so.

Spock, Dr. McCoy, and I will return shortly to the planet's surface to join the crew presently on rotation there. It is hoped we will gather additional information.

Lieutenant Uhura sat with Kelly Davis at the edge of a large, grassy park. The tree they leaned against towered above them, its twisted branches swaying slightly in the breeze. The sky was a strange shade of blue-green, flaked with high, scattered clouds. It was peaceful in the park, quiet, uncrowded. The *Enterprise* was far from their minds.

It was a good place to rest, take a small breather. Things had been busy, they'd worked hard for months. Now there was a small time for relaxation, letting go.

Uhura, feeling the soft winds she hadn't felt in months, began to sing softly to herself. The words were in Bantu, the rhythm gentle. They were old words, from older times.

"What is that?" asked Kelly lazily.

"Ummm . . . an old song about the children of the moon, and the lions they meet on the path to glory. It's a nonsense song, meant for putting small children to sleep. I learned it sitting on the lap of my mother's mother. It was an old song even then."

"We had songs like that on my planet, too," said Kelly. "I dreamed of one last night—ships on a golden sea. It seemed real."

"Where did you grow up?" asked Uhuru.

"A planet called New Enid."

"I've heard of that. It's a desert planet, isn't it?"

Kelly laughed. "You might call it that, most people do. It never really seemed that way to me, it was home, that's all. Kids don't seem to mind things like that as much as adults. Of course I remember the heat, but even more I remember the coolness of my bedroom, the rustle of the prickly-bush outside my window. I was just a child at the time."

"You left, then?" asked Uhura.

"My parents were killed by a sickness that swept the colony. I went to live with my Uncle Joe, who taught astronomy at the university on Ponca II. I was only ten at the time. He saw I got a good, basic education. When I graduated from the med school at the university, I was only nineteen, the youngest doctor on the planet. Of course I was highly motivated. I went into virology . . ." her voice trailed off. She paused. "For my parents, I guess."

"I can understand that," said Uhura.

"I've never been able to stay put, settle down. Seems like I've been on the move ever since then. People keep trying to stick me in a lab somewhere, to teach, do basic research. But I want to work with *people*. If they put me behind a desk, I'd die."

"I know what you mean," said Uhura, "Life on the *Enterprise* can get pretty hectic, but I wouldn't trade it for anything." She paused, smiled. "Well, *almost* anything."

"I suppose if the right man came along, you might reconsider?" asked Kelly with a laugh.

"It's a possibility," grinned Uhura. "A distinct possibility."

They leaned back, relaxed, watching the other people in the park, mostly couples. They were the only two from the *Enterprise* in sight. The park was a remote one, at the edge of the city. They had chosen it for just that reason. Uhura had been feeling hemmed in lately. Kelly was good company.

"I came close to that route once," said Kelly. "His name was Mike and he was a good man, but—"

Uhura grabbed her arm. *"Look!"*

At the edge of the park a man was dragging a woman toward an overgrown path. She was struggling, but not much. As they watched, she went limp in his arms.

"Let's go," said Uhura, jumping to her feet. Kelly held her back.

"Wait," she said. "We don't know anything about the culture here. That could be normal courtship ritual. I've seen worse on a dozen different planets."

"You can't be serious," said Uhura.

"Look around," said Kelly. "Nobody is doing anything at all."

It was true. The other people in the park were behaving just as they had before. Nobody paid any attention at all as the man disappeared into the underbrush half carrying, half dragging the unconscious woman.

"I think we'd better get in touch with the Captain," said Uhura.

It wasn't possible, Scotty told her, not at this time. The Captain was in conference on the planet's surface and had left word not to be disturbed unless absolutely necessary. They decided that it could wait. In the meantime they left the park to seek out whatever passed for the local police department.

Neither woman had noticed the man was scruffily dressed, that he wore no scarf.

The wooden sign swung in the breeze above the door. *The Crossroads Tavern* it read, embellished with a rough drawing of a glass of beer and a plate of food. Ami had recommended the pub to Kirk, and they sat at a table in the back with McCoy and Spock. Other crewmen from the *Enterprise* were in the establishment, eating, drinking, and mingling with the local people. A trio of stringed instruments was playing on a raised platform by the bar. The air was filled with good music, quiet conversation, and soft laughter. Kirk felt the friendly atmosphere and tried to relax.

"How long have you been a page?" he asked, sipping his beer. It was served warm, but tasted fine.

"Since I was twelve," said Ami. "It is customary on Perry to pledge an apprenticeship before your thirteenth birthday. My father had been a member of the Council, so it was natural, though not required, that I pledge my services to them. I have not regretted it."

"Will you automatically become a Council member someday?" asked McCoy. He was finally out of his dress uniform and feeling a lot more comfortable.

"No," said Ami. "It doesn't work that way. There are many pages, but only a very few of them will be elected to Council seats. The rest will serve in a variety of other ways, ranging from advisory positions to dealing with the paperwork. There's always a lot of paperwork."

Kirk laughed. "I've noticed that's true on almost every planet. People and paper just seem to go together. It seems like there must be some sort of a symbiotic relationship between humans and forms printed on paper."

"I know what you mean," said Ami. "But it's not as bad here as it could be. Computers take care of most of that for us."

Spock and Kirk looked at each other.

"Do you have a lot of computers here?" asked Kirk, keeping his voice calm and conversational.

"Yes, I think so. Or maybe they're all branches of one big computer. I'm not sure. They keep track of a lot of things; our credit system, for example."

"I noticed you don't use any form of money here," said McCoy. "How does that work?"

Ami fumbled in a pouch she carried and pulled out a small plastic disk, passed it to McCoy. "Each of us has a disk like this," she said. "The computer codes it with a credit for the amount of work we do. When we purchase anything, the amount is subtracted from our total balance. The computer does it all. We

45

never really know our exact balance. The disk is supposed to turn orange if our account is low, but I've never seen it happen to anyone."

McCoy passed the disk back. "It sounds complicated," he said.

"It isn't, really. We never think about it. The computer handles everything."

"It appears you must have a pretty sophisticated computer system," said Kirk.

"I guess it is," said Ami. "I don't know very much about it, though. You'd have to ask a Red about it, or maybe a Blue. They'd know."

"I suppose Captain Perry would know, too," said Kirk.

"Oh yes," said Ami. "Perry knows just about everything."

"Everything?"

"Of course," said Ami. "He ought to, he's our ruler. They're supposed to know everything, or they wouldn't be rulers. That's obvious."

"Has anyone but Captain Perry ever ruled this planet?" asked Kirk.

Ami looked puzzled. "What a silly thing to ask. Of course Perry is our only ruler. There is only one Wayne Perry. It would be ridiculous to have more than one, don't you think?"

"Certainly illogical," said McCoy with a wry look toward Spock.

"If that's an attempt at humor," said Spock dryly, "I fail to see the point of it."

"You wouldn't," said McCoy.

Kirk turned to Ami. "What works on one planet doesn't necessary work for others. Some planets, most of them, change their leaders quite often."

"Why would they want to do a thing like that?"

"Many reasons," said Kirk. "Some people feel it makes their leaders more responsive to the public and its needs."

"That doesn't make any sense at all," said Ami. "A leader has to do what is good for the people, even if they don't always understand it. That's what a leader is for. He knows more than the people and he's wiser, so he always knows what to do."

"Always?" asked Kirk.

Ami nodded seriously. "Always," she said.

"Even good leaders die," said Kirk.

Ami blinked, sat back sharply. "Why would they do that? Leaders don't die."

"Do you think they live forever?"

"Wayne Perry does," she said firmly.

"How can you believe that?" Kirk asked.

"There are many things I don't understand," she said. "But I am a good citizen and a good citizen does not question the things that are. Wayne Perry led the Council when my father was a boy and his father before that. That is the way it is and has always been."

A harsh noise diverted Kirk's attention. He looked toward a table in the front of the room and saw Sulu in an animated discussion with Wade Moody, a machinist's mate. Sulu looked irritated.

McCoy touched Kirk's arm. "Looks like a little steam is going to be let off," he said.

Kirk nodded. He wasn't surprised at all. The strain the crew had been under was bound to show itself here and there. It wouldn't hurt to let the two of them pound it out a little, but not here. It would create a bad impression on the local inhabitants. They'd be better working it out in the gym aboard ship.

"Excuse me a second," he said to Ami, rising from his chair.

As he left the table, he saw that he was already too late. Sulu was standing, his face a mask of anger, his arm drawn back in readiness to swing at Wade. The swing was never completed.

Suddenly Sulu's face went totally blank, devoid of

any expression whatsoever. He fell to the floor in a limp heap, as if he had been a puppet whose strings had been cut.

"Bones," shouted Kirk.

McCoy was already on his feet, his chair flying out behind him. Together they rushed toward Sulu. The crew members in the pub had grown quiet, concerned about their fallen comrade. The trio unexplainably continued to play, the natives remained casual, looked the other way, studiously ignoring the situation.

McCoy gave Sulu a quick examination. The young man looked pale, his breathing was shallow.

"Jim," said McCoy. "He's in deep shock. I've got to move fast."

Kirk flipped open his communicator. "Kirk to *Enterprise*," he said sharply.

"Scott here, sir."

"Medical emergency, Scotty. Get a fix on the three of us. Beam us aboard. Quickly."

"Aye, sir."

Kirk looked at McCoy bent over Sulu's unmoving form. Sulu's eyes were open, but unseeing. He seemed to be drifting away. Kirk had seen death many times and once again he felt the beat of black, leathery wings. *Why?*

And this was going to be one of the easy ones.

The room faded away.

CHAPTER SIX

As Kirk, McCoy, and Sulu materialized on the transporter platform, two nurses rushed into the room, pushing a stretcher. McCoy and Kirk lifted Sulu's limp form and swung him onto it.

McCoy bent over Sulu, waving the medical tricorder over his body. His face was set in a hard frown.

"I don't understand this, Jim," he said. "A minute ago he was dying—I'm sure of that—and now—"

Sulu sat up, looked around him. His eyes were dazed, but clearing rapidly. "What . . . ? How did I get here? Is this some kind of a joke?"

"Take it easy, Mr. Sulu," said Kirk. "You were out cold a minute ago." *Dying,* he thought, but did not say, *dying.*

"What are you talking about? I feel fine."

"Readings are all normal, Jim. Looks like the same switch that turned him off so quickly turned him on again."

"Any ideas?"

"None. None at all. I'll want to take him to sick bay and check him out completely, of course. I'll have some tests to run." He shook his head. "Lots of tests."

"Sick bay?" asked Sulu. "Have you all lost your minds? There's nothing wrong with me."

"Suppose we let the good doctor be the judge of that, Mr. Sulu," said Kirk. "What do you remember of the incident?"

"What incident? I was talking to Moody and the

next thing I knew I was up here with this crazy doctor poking at me."

"You don't remember the fight?" asked Kirk. "Or the argument?"

Sulu shook his head. "There was no argument, certainly no fight. We were having a couple of drinks and some quiet conversation."

Kirk and McCoy looked at each other, shook their heads. McCoy frowned, put away the tricorder.

"I'd like to get started on those tests as soon as possible," he said.

"Do that, Bones," said Kirk. "And when you're finished get in touch with me right away. I have some questions for Mr. Sulu when you're through. I'd be very much interested in his answers."

McCoy and the nurses started to wheel Sulu out of the transporter room.

"I'd rather walk," said Sulu.

"And I'd rather you'd just ride along," said McCoy. "You may still be a little shaky."

"I'm fine," said Sulu. "There's nothing wrong with me." He pulled off the restraints that held him to the stretcher. McCoy reached down to replace them and Sulu made a quick grab toward his arm.

Abruptly, the anger drained from Sulu's face. It was replaced by a blank stare. He fell heavily back against the padded stretcher, his face drained.

"He's done it again," said McCoy. "Sick bay. On the double."

Rapidly, they rolled him from the transporter room.

"May I ask what all that was aboot, Captain?" said Scott. "He went doon verra fast."

"I don't know what it's about, Scotty. But I'm going to find out. Prepare to beam me back down."

"Do you expect trouble, sir?"

"I don't know what to expect. Something's wrong, though. That's all I know."

McCoy's voice came over the intercom. "McCoy to transporter room."

Scott slapped the panel. "Transporter room. Scott here."

"Has the Captain left yet?"

"I'm still here, Bones," said Kirk, stepping from the platform toward the intercom. "What is it?"

"It's Sulu, Jim. He's back to normal again. He recovered before we even got to sick bay. Doesn't remember a thing about it."

"Okay. I'm beaming back down. Keep me posted."

"I'll do that, Jim. The tests might show something, but frankly, I'm worried. I don't like attacks that come and go, leaving no traces. It's hard to figure."

"I know, Bones. It worried me, too."

"Be careful, Jim. We don't know what we're dealing with."

"That's all I *am* sure of. Kirk out." He stepped on the transporter platform, nodded to Scotty. "Energize," he said.

"Aye, sir," said Scotty, thinking of the earlier report he'd gotten from Uhura and Kelly. The Captain seemed a little preoccupied for that now. It would probably be better to bring it up later. He moved the levers and the Captain disappeared.

Kirk materialized on the sidewalk outside the pub, immediately rushed inside. Spock was standing at the rear table, talking with Ami. He went back to join them. Spock stepped away from the table, intercepted him.

"I thought we might best speak out of the hearing range of the woman Ami," said Spock.

"What is it, Mr. Spock? Do you have a report?"

"Yes, Captain, a preliminary one. One of considerable negative information."

"How so?"

"We have here a most peculiar set of circumstances. Although we clearly saw Mr. Sulu arguing with Mr. Moody up to the point of physical violence, it appears that we were alone in observing this."

"Get to the point, Spock."

"The point is, Captain, that I have been unable to find anyone, other than the crew, who will admit to having seen the altercation. Mr. Moody concurs that he and Mr. Sulu were exchanging words and Mr. Sulu threatened to—I think the phrase was 'punch him out.' This would correspond to the events as we witnessed them, but the two natives at the table with them deny any such event transpired."

"They deny it? We saw it with our own eyes."

"So it would seem. They are not alone in their interpretation of the events, however. There were eighty-seven inhabitants of Perry in this building at the time that Mr. Sulu collapsed. Enlisting the aid of Mr. Huff and Mr. Bischoff we managed to question all but one of them. None of them admit to seeing anything."

"Your opinion, Mr. Spock?"

"There are many possibilities, but only three major ones. One: that they did see the altercation, but chose not to admit it. Two: that they truly did not see the event. Three: that the event did not occur as we believe we observed it."

"Your analysis?"

"The third possibility must be assigned a very low probability. It is highly unlikely that all the members of the *Enterprise* in this establishment would simultaneously hallucinate the same event. The second possibility is only slightly better. The restaurant is crowded, the people have eyes and ears. Mr. Sulu's voice was raised to a degree that we heard it at the back of the room. It would be hard to imagine that this could go totally unnoticed by so many people. The first possibility looks to be the most likely. After interviewing the people, I am inclined to accept it, with one reservation."

"What reservation?"

"That they may not be unwilling to talk about it, they may be *unable* to."

"Unable? That's ridiculous, Mr. Spock."

"Indeed?" asked Spock. "I am not usually given to ridiculous statements. I suggest you conduct your own investigation. A suitable subject is available at the table." He indicated Ami, sitting with Rus, who had apparently joined them. Their conversation seemed casual.

"You mentioned you questioned all but one person," said Kirk. "Why not that one?"

"I'm glad you asked that, Captain," said Spock, leaning back and folding his arms. "That one person was quite unusual."

"In what way?"

"He wore no scarf, no badge of office. He wore clothes that superficially resembled the rather unimaginative attire of the others, but they were frayed and tattered."

"Why didn't you mention it at the time?"

"I was waiting for the chance. As you will recall, we were interrupted."

"I recall that, Mr. Spock," said Kirk, a note of exasperation creeping into his voice. "But why didn't you question him afterward?"

"Simply because he left during the altercation."

"Didn't you think that unusual?"

"Not especially. The fight was of no concern to him. He removed himself from danger. That is only surprising in retrospect."

"How so?"

"He was the only native of Perry to do so. All the others do not even admit to having seen the altercation."

53

"I think I had better talk with Ami," said Kirk.

"That would seem to be indicated," said Spock, trailing as they headed for the table.

"I'm sorry for the interruption of our dinner," Kirk said.

"That's quite all right," said Ami. "I'm sure the captain of a starship must be quite similar to a ruler on a planet. You must be very busy."

"Sometimes just keeping an eye on my crew occupies most of my time. Like what just happened."

"And how's that?" asked Ami, raising her water glass.

"Averting fights, things like that. You understand."

"No. I don't understand."

"My crew has been under a lot of stress lately. It wouldn't be too unusual for them to take it out on each other once in a while."

"Take it out? I don't know what that means."

"Fight. Quarrel. Push each other around."

"No. They won't do that. Not here."

"It almost happened, right here in this room. Two of my men nearly got into a fight. Something stopped them."

"I saw nothing."

"It happened nonetheless."

She shook her head, stared at Kirk over the rim of her water glass. Her eyes were deep blue. "There is no violence on Perry," she said calmly. "We are a peaceful people."

"I'm talking about my people, not yours," he said.

"It doesn't matter," she said. "It is impossible, even for your people. There is *no violence* at all on Perry."

"What is that, some kind of a rule?"

She looked at him for a long second. If there was any deceit behind her eyes it was hidden from Kirk. "It is not a rule, it is a way of life."

Spock's voice in his ear was even, devoid of emotion. "Vital signs steady, Captain. No signs of galvanic skin responses, changes in heart rate, or increased vasoconstriction. She is telling the truth. There is no doubt about it."

"Of course she's telling the truth," said Rus. "You will find that we on Perry are a very peaceful people, a society totally devoid of violence."

Impossible, thought Kirk, impossible. The answer must be with Wayne Perry, whatever he is.

Kirk's communicator beeped. He removed it from his belt, flipped it open.

"Kirk here."

"Jim, you and Spock had better get up here right away. We've got big trouble."

"What is it, Bones?"

"I'm not sure, but I think whatever Sulu has is spreading. It may be too late to stop it."

"We'll be right up. Kirk out." He looked at Spock. "It looks like we have another problem," he said. "This planet is full of them."

"So it would seem," said Spock.

It had been building for a long time, starting back with a dispute over a card game. There was also a woman, apparently playing the two men against each other. The whole issue was clouded by feelings of anger, jealousy, and dislike. They had things to get out of their system and decided to do it in the gymnasium.

Two falls out of three.

They faced each other across the padded mat. It was a fairly even match—they were both strong, large, in good shape. A referee, a mutual friend, stood by. It was unlikely they would need him except to time the match.

"Start," he said.

The two men circled the mat for a second, then—at the same instant—they lunged at each other. They never met.

Both collapsed suddenly, twitched a couple of times

and were still. The referee stood in shock. The first thing that crossed his mind was that they had both suffered simultaneous heart attacks. At the same time he knew that didn't make sense. He ran to the wall, slapped the intercom.

"A medical team to the gym," he shouted. "Hurry."

It had started.

CHAPTER SEVEN

Ship's Medical Log, McCoy Recording, Stardate 6836.2:

Nurse Chapel and I have just completed an extensive physical examination of Mr. Sulu. Aside from a minor scrape on the chin, accidently incurred on the planet Perry, there are no detectable signs of physical abnormalities at all. Following an observation by Mr. Spock that Mr. Sulu's two episodes of unconsciousness were preceded by uncompleted acts of violence, we arranged a small experiment. An attempt was made to induce hostile action from Mr. Sulu. This proved unexpectedly difficult. Even when provoked, he exhibited no violent tendencies. It was necessary to refer to his confidential psychological report in order to produce an area sensitive enough to evoke a response from him. This was as unpleasant for me as it was for the patient. *(NOTE: Refer at later date that Star Fleet Command reevaluate procedures for classification of psychological data. I don't feel that even I should have such ready access to data this personal.)* After appropriate stimulus—a reference to a buried traumatic and humiliating event—Mr. Sulu again attempted a violent act and lapsed into an unconscious state. We monitored this condition with all the facilities available. He instantly slipped into a state of deep shock. His vital signs dropped suddenly and drastically. His respiration rate was undetectable, his heart beat only once every five seconds. He was, by all measurable signs, very near death. I stood by ready to revive him, but it was not necessary. His recovery was as sudden as his collapse. He was in a state of shock for a total of seventeen seconds and suffered, as nearly as we could tell, no ill effects at all. Five seconds after regaining consciousness all his vital signs were perfectly normal, no signs of stress remained. It was as if he had just awakened from a deep, restful sleep. He remembered nothing of the incident. Each of his episodes of unconsciousness have been progressively shorter and more difficult to induce. I would suspect it would be almost impossible to produce another one in this patient. It is almost as if he had been conditioned. Conditioned against violence.

There have been, as of this date, four similar incidents aboard the *Enterprise.*

They gathered in McCoy's office. There were four of them: McCoy, Kirk, Spock, and Kelly Davis. The mood was somber, deadly serious. There had been two more incidents.

"We're all agreed, I take it, that these periods of unconsciousness are preceded by acts of uncompleted violence?" asked Kirk.

"We seem to know the 'what,' but not the 'how' or the 'why,' " said McCoy.

"It's an intriguing situation," said Spock. "When I observed the woman, Ami was telling the truth that there was no violence on Perry, I had formed a hypothesis of some sort of psychological conditioning or patterning. That however, could not have affected Sulu or the rest of the crew so soon. Regrettably, I had to abandon the hypothesis. It was an interesting one. Unfortunately it is no longer valid."

"Your invalid hypothesis is all very interesting, Mr. Spock, but we need some valid ones." Kirk's voice was sharper than he had intended, his frustration was showing.

"I was simply discussing a discarded line of reasoning, Captain."

"I *know* that, Spock," said Kirk. "What we need are valid lines of reasoning."

"I wish I'd never brought Sulu up to the ship," said McCoy. "But it seemed like the thing to do at the time."

"It was the correct procedure," said Spock. "There was no reason for you, or any of us, to expect that it was contagious."

"That, in fact, is about the only thing we do know," said Kelly. "It acts like a psychoactive virus, but we haven't been able to pin it down."

"Psychoactive virus?" asked Kirk. "What's that?"

"Fascinating," said Spock. "It would fit all the parameters we have so far observed."

"It's just that we have no solid evidence," said McCoy. "If it's a virus, it's a damn sneaky one."

"Will somebody tell me what's going on?" asked Kirk in exasperation.

"That would explain the rapid transmission," said Kelly. "Since some of the people exhibiting the symptoms have never been on the planet's surface, it seems logical that Sulu brought it up. Or we may have all brought it up, for that matter."

"That's quite possible," said Spock. "The probability is quite high that we are all infected."

"Stop. *Stop!*" shouted Kirk. "Will someone *please* explain to me what this is you're talking about. What is this infected business? Is some germ causing all this? Bones?"

"Not a germ, exactly, Jim, but a virus. And we're not sure that's the correct answer at all, but it fits the data better than anything else we've come up with. Like I said, though, we don't have any concrete evidence for it."

"You said it was a psycho . . ." Kirk searched for the word.

"Psychoactive virus, Captain," said Kelly. "That's kind of a loose term for a virus with psychological effects."

"How does it work?"

"We're just guessing," said McCoy, "but if it is a virus it's probably dormant, or inactive, until something triggers it. In this case, we think it may be reacting to a change in the body chemistry associated with rage or violence. When it senses those changes in the body's normal chemical balance, it fires itself up and shuts the body down. Temporarily, thank goodness."

"I've seen something similar using gasses," said Kirk. "A cat chasing a mouse will suddenly turn in terror when it gets a whiff of the gas."

"We thought it might be something like that in the planet's atmosphere at first," said McCoy, "but when it spread through the ship, we pretty much had to rule it out. A gas wouldn't work that way. A virus might."

"It's extremely adaptive, whatever it is," said Kelly. "So far it hasn't shown up on any of our tests."

"But if it's there, we'll find it," said McCoy. "I'd like to try some cultures and more sophisticated tests, but first I had better get a more substantial baseline."

"How's that?" asked Kirk.

"I'd like to run some preliminary tests on the natives of this planet. It might give us a better idea where to start."

"I'm sure that could be arranged. I have a few questions for them myself," Kirk said bitterly. "How long will it take you to get your equipment ready?"

"We don't need much. It's ready now."

"Good. Let's go."

In the rush of things, Kelly had forgotten to mention to Kirk about the violence she had observed on Perry. It didn't seem as important as the work they were doing. It could wait.

When they arrived on the planet's surface, they split into two groups. McCoy and Kelly Davis went to look for suitable subjects to test and Spock and Kirk headed for the Council Chambers.

The building seemed deserted, the only member in the chamber was Jon, the eldest one. He greeted them warmly and pleasantly. Kirk was in no mood for small talk.

"I wish to talk with Wayne Perry," he said.

"Impossible," said Jon. "Quite impossible at this time. He is a busy man and presently his attentions are elsewhere."

"I don't care how busy he is, I've got to speak with him," said Kirk.

Jon shrugged. "I don't see what good it will do, but I'll put your request through to him. He may or may not respond."

Jon pushed aside a panel recessed on the table in front of him, revealing a keyboard and a small screen. It was obviously a computer access terminal. Spock looked questioningly at Kirk as Jon tapped the keys.

"He will see you shortly," said Jon, sliding the panel back into place. "In the meantime, why not make yourselves comfortable?"

"I don't want to be comfortable," snapped Kirk. "What I want to know is what's happening on this crazy planet."

"Indeed," said Jon with a faint smile. "What leads you to believe that this is a 'crazy planet'? We who live here consider it a pleasant place, a calm place."

"My men are dropping like flies," said Kirk.

"If they were not violent, that would not happen," said Jon. "We on Perry have learned how to control our violent impulses, we live in peace."

"I still find that difficult, if not impossible, to believe," said Kirk. "All I see are your smiling faces as my men collapse all around me."

"We are a very peaceful people. Soon you will be like us and then you will understand."

"We don't want to be like you. We *can't* be like you. I'm not convinced your way of life is practical even in a closed society like you have on Perry. It would be disastrous for us."

"Would it, Captain? Really? I think you will feel different when the whole universe learns to live in peace. There will be no need for violence. I am an old man, yet I may live to see that day."

"All I know is that my crew seems to be infected with a strange disease and *you* gave it to them."

"Has anyone died? Has anyone been seriously injured?"

"No," admitted Kirk. "But it could only be a matter of time."

"I seriously doubt that," said Jon.

"I don't," said Kirk, "not for a minute. This could turn out to be deadlier to mankind than the plague on Altair IV."

Jon shook his head. "I suppose you issue tranquilizers on your ship. They calm people, keep them from violent acts. Would you call a tranquilizer deadly?"

"Yes, under certain conditions," said Kirk. "It could prevent a person from functioning properly in a dangerous situation."

"You miss the point," said Jon. "Violence can not be tolerated in a nonviolent society. We must all learn to live in peace."

"But we *don't* live in a nonviolent society," said Kirk.

"You will," said Jon. "Very soon."

At that moment McCoy rushed into the Council Chamber. His uniform was torn, blood was running down the side of his face from a ragged cut above his left eye.

"Bones," shouted Kirk. "What happened?"

"Never mind me," he said hurriedly. "Scotty's been trying to reach you. They can't—"

"This building's shielded," said Kirk. "We'll have to go outside."

"Hurry," said McCoy.

Spock took McCoy's arm and the three of them headed for the door.

"Ship attacked—Klingons," gasped McCoy as they stepped outside.

CHAPTER EIGHT

Kirk flipped open his communicator. "Kirk to *Enterprise.*" The sky overhead was clear, the breeze calm. Everything about the planet seemed calm on the surface, Kirk thought, but deadly underneath.

"Scott here, sir. Thank goodness we reached you. It's bad here, verra bad."

"Bring me up to date," said Kirk, more calmly than he felt, trying to keep Scotty from getting any more excited or panicked than he already was. It was an understandable reaction on Scotty's part, but it couldn't help the situation at all.

"Klingons, sir. Korol and his bunch. Right out of nowhere. I don't think they were lookin' for us though, they're probably as surprised as we are. We saw them comin' in plenty of time to erect our deflector shields. If they'd been after us, we never would ha'e seen 'em."

"I can believe that," said Kirk, half to himself.

"They fired a couple o' shots, but we deflected them okay." He paused. "Sir, we don't have enough power to run and . . ."

"They fired on us first, Scotty. That's open aggression. Why don't you . . ." Kirk trailed off, his voice shaky. He was struck by a sudden wave of dizziness. He looked over at Spock, who was dressing McCoy's scalp wound.

"Spock! I can't even *give* an offensive order."

Spock shook his head. "I'm sure they couldn't carry it out even if you could order it."

Scotty's voice came through the communicator. He sounded weary—and frightened. "I heard that, sir. It's true. None of us can get near the phaser controls. We've tried, but it canna' be done."

"I understand, Scotty."

"We dare not drop the shields, sir." He paused. "Besides yourself, there are over a dozen crewmen down there. Uhura . . ." His voice trailed off. "I'm afraid . . ."

"I realize you can't use the transporter. That's unfortunate, but necessary. Do what you can. We'll do whatever is possible down here. Just hold on."

"Aye, sir."

Neither of them mentioned the failing dilithium crystals. That was the limiting factor and they both knew it only too well. How long the crystals lasted would determine how long the shields could be maintained, how long the *Enterprise* could fight even a holding action. Kirk estimated about three to four hours under full shields, but he could be wrong about that. Quite wrong.

As soon as Kirk finished talking with Scott, he turned back into the building, headed straight for the Council Chambers. McCoy, his bleeding stopped, and Spock followed him.

Much to their surprise, Wayne Perry was waiting for them. He was alone. Jon had evidently been sent elsewhere. Kirk could barely control his anger and frustration. He had to get to the bottom of this and quickly.

"I'm sorry I wasn't here to meet you earlier," said Perry, "but I hadn't expected you so soon. I was occupied with other business."

"Talking to the Klingons, no doubt," said Kirk.

"As a matter of fact, no," said Perry with a smile.

"The Klingon ship has been much too busy since their arrival to contact me. I suspect they will get around to it in due time. There is no need to rush them."

"Did you call them to Perry in order to be trapped like we are?" asked Kirk.

Perry shrugged. "What difference would that make? You are violent men. Where violent men go, violent men follow. They would have been here sooner or later." He paused, stood from his chair. "Actually, I did contact them, much as I contacted you. But I would hardly call you trapped. You are free to leave at any time."

"Free to leave?" Kirk asked incredulously. "Thanks to the Klingons we couldn't leave even if we wanted to."

"That's not my problem," said Perry. "Violence begets violence. Someday you will all live in a totally peaceful universe and then, perhaps, you will realize the folly of your previous ways."

"I've heard that line before, and I still don't believe it," said Kirk. "What have you done to my men?"

"Me? Nothing at all. Well, *almost* nothing at all. Let's just say they have caught the peaceful spirit of our planet."

"I'd say they've caught something else. Something potentially deadly. Something that impairs their ability to defend themselves."

"They are *not* impaired," said Perry firmly. "Violence is not a necessary attribute of humanity. In fact, it is not even desirable. On this planet we have eliminated it once and for all. Soon it will spread."

"What if we don't leave?" asked Kirk. "What if we choose to stay rather than spread this nightmare to other planets?"

"That is of little concern to me. You came, the Klingons came. There will be others. Our word of peace will spread."

"Your *disease* will spread," snapped Kirk.

"Hardly a disease, Captain. I prefer to think of it as a *cure* to a disease, a disease as old as mankind. Throughout history violence has always stood in the way of man's reaching higher goals. This is the perfect solution to that."

"Hardly perfect," said McCoy bitterly. "Even on your own planet."

Perry and Kirk turned to look at McCoy. Spock sat calmly beside him, taking everything in.

"Dr. McCoy, isn't it?" said Perry. "I'm sure I don't understand what you mean."

"There are people on this planet that are plenty capable of violence of all sorts." He touched the side of his head gingerly. "I just had a run-in with one of them. How does an attack with a blunt instrument sound for violence? Or kidnapping?"

"What?" said Kirk.

"Somebody hit me. When I came around, Kelly Davis was gone. I can only assume they took her. She would never have left me there on her own."

"You are certainly mistaken, Dr. McCoy," said Perry. "Nothing of the sort could have happened on this planet. I suggest that you are confused. Perhaps your head injury—probably an accident—has impaired your mental processes. You are most likely hallucinating."

"I most certainly am not," said McCoy.

"Perhaps you need time to rest. I am sure that Captain Kirk could use some time to calm down. Soon he will see the reasoning behind what is happening, you all will. Until then, I believe further discussion is futile. This audience is terminated."

Abruptly, Wayne Perry turned and exited through the side door to the chambers. It closed with a heavy thud.

"I believe we've been dismissed," said Spock.

"So it would appear," said Kirk and they left.

A quick check with Scotty showed that the situation aboard the *Enterprise* hadn't changed much. Random fire from the Klingon vessel was forcing them to keep the ship's shields at full strength. It looked bad. Kirk turned to McCoy.

"How do you feel, Bones?"

"I'm afraid I'll live, Jim. But I know what I saw, I'm sure of it. I didn't hallucinate this bump on my head. He was five feet ten, over two hundred pounds. I saw him, I know I did."

"Take it easy, Bones. We believe you."

"How was he dressed?" asked Spock.

McCoy and Kirk turned to him, puzzled. It was sometimes difficult to see what Spock was getting at.

"What possible difference could that make?" asked Kirk.

"It could make a considerable difference," said Spock. "Did you notice anything unusual about your assailant, Dr. McCoy?"

"It happened so fast. I remember he was kind of scruffy, not very well dressed, something like that."

"Did he wear a scarf, a badge of office?"

McCoy shook his head slowly. "I don't think so. No, I'm almost sure he didn't. If he had, I would have remembered the color."

"What are you getting at, Mr. Spock?" asked Kirk.

"It occurs to me that we have two anomalies here— examples of behavior that don't fit the normal pattern of life on Perry, at least as we understand it at this time. I am trying to connect them."

"In what way?"

"The man who attacked Dr. McCoy and the man who left the pub when Mr. Sulu's altercation began both exhibit signs of behavior we would not expect from natives on Perry. Furthermore, neither of them wore the traditional scarves. It would appear that

they exist outside the mainstream of Perry's supposed-
ly smooth-running society. More to the point, at least
the one who attacked Dr. McCoy is capable of violence. That in itself is highly significant. It would bear
investigation."

"We don't have *time* for anything like that, Spock,"
snapped Kirk. "I don't know how long Scotty can hold
out. We're running out of time all over the place."

"Easy, Jim," said McCoy.

"For once I agree with Dr. McCoy," said Spock.
"We all realize that the ship is in a bad situation. We
must also realize that we are not on board and we
cannot get aboard while her shields are up. Therefore
the matter, for better or for worse, is in the hands of
Mr. Scott."

"What do you suggest that's any better?" asked
Kirk sharply. "Go chasing after any people we see
who don't wear scarves or who look unusual?"

"That would be one avenue of approach, though
perhaps not the most productive one at this time."

"You have a better idea?" asked Kirk sarcastically.

"I think so, Captain," said Spock. "It seems to me
that in trying to deal with Wayne Perry we may have
been missing the point."

"What point?"

"That Wayne Perry is a computer construct. We
might do better dealing with the computer directly."

"Do you think that's possible?" asked McCoy. "We
don't even have any idea where the computer is, much
less how it functions."

"It's possible," nodded Spock, "but it may be difficult. The computer may or may not be centralized; it
is certainly hidden. The only interfaces to it I have
seen have been in the Council chambers."

"Then that's the place to start," said Kirk.

"I don't think so, Captain. Both the door that Wayne
Perry uses and the panel that Jon contacted him with

are protected by complex locking devices. It would, in all probability, take several days to deduce the code by trial and error."

"So where do you suggest we start looking?" asked McCoy.

Spock pointed down at the sidewalk. "I believe the answer is beneath our feet."

"I think you're the one who got knocked on the head," said McCoy.

"No," said Kirk. "He might have something there."

Spock nodded, ignoring McCoy's comment. "Dr. McCoy may not be aware that there are areas beneath the city that are shielded in such a manner as to prevent analysis by tricorder. It is apparently a system of interlocking tunnels. What sparse readings we have been able to obtain indicate computer activity, among other signs."

"What other signs?" asked McCoy.

"Signs of life," said Spock. "Evidently humanoid life."

"Wayne Perry never mentioned that, nor did Ami," said McCoy.

"Precisely the point, Doctor."

"Spock may be right," said Kirk. "It isn't likely that Perry would admit to his mistakes. If there are people on this planet unaffected by whatever has hit us, it's likely they might be there. Also the central computer."

"It would seem logical," said Spock.

"So where do we start?" asked McCoy.

"We start by keeping our eyes open," said Spock evenly, unhooking the tricorder.

Kelly Davis opened her eyes slowly. Everything was blurry, her head hurt. She moved her fingers, legs, arms. Everything seemed to work, nothing was broken. *Thanks for small favors,* she thought. Still dizzy, the room spun around her, everything out of focus.

"Kelly." A whispered voice. Familiar.

She blinked twice, focused with a conscious effort. A face took form. "Uhura," she said.

"Shush," said Uhura, raising a finger to her lips. "They might hear you." Her left eye was swollen shut.

"Who?" asked Kelly.

Uhura shuddered, and Kelly followed her gaze to the doorway.

Three men stood there, ragged, brutish. They wore no scarves. Without consciously noticing the knives and blunt clubs they carried, Kelly was instantly aware they were quite capable of violence. Any kind of violence.

She was right.

CHAPTER NINE

Ship's Log, Lieutenant Commander Scott Recording, Stardate 6845.3:

The situation remains critical. There seems to be nothing we can do but maintain a defensive posture. Even that is limited by the failing dilithium crystals. It is no longer possible even to leave or change orbit while maintaining the shields at the necessary level. As long as the Klingons continue their sporadic firing, we are helpless.

In addition, contact has been lost with Lieutenant Uhura. According to reports from the planet's surface, Dr. Davis is also missing. Since she was not issued a communicator, she cannot be traced from the ship.

An attempt has been made to jury-rig the phaser controls so that they could be triggered without conscious thought. It was a miserable failure and cost us considerable time.

Our position is deteriorating rapidly. We are running out of options.

Scotty's burly frame filled the Captain's chair. He felt as uncomfortable as he looked. With all his heart and soul he wished that Kirk was in the chair and he was back in his familar engine room.

He'd never wanted command, but had accepted it willingly when it was forced upon him. There had been other times when he had found himself in command of the ship, and he had been trained for it, but this was different. Now he had no control over the situation, was unable to do what every fiber in his body screamed to do—fight.

He tapped the intercom open. "Bridge to Engineerin'."

"Nason here, sir."

"Give me an update on the crystals."

"Not good, sir. We're approaching the decay point. It will go rapidly downhill from there."

"I suppose you've tried a shunt from the auxiliary patch board?"

"Yes, sir. As you would expect, we got nothing. The delta figures are getting smaller."

"A time estimate?"

"Roughly an hour, maybe two. The decay factor is unpredictable until it starts. I'll have a better idea in about twenty minutes."

"Carry on, Nason. Let me have the revised estimate when you get it."

"Yes, sir."

"Bridge out."

Scotty resisted the urge to head back to Engineering. Although it was irrational, he couldn't help thinking that his mere presence would help things. He'd squeeze the extra ergs out of the crystals with his bare hands if it was possible. Nason was a good man, he was undoubtedly doing everything that could be done. There was nothing Scotty could do back there that would help. Frustration overwhelmed him.

The Klingon ship hung in the viewscreen, the planet's mottled surface below it. Scotty clenched his teeth, wondering how Korol would savor the victory when it came.

Korol was a renegade. By swearing the blood oath against Kirk and blatantly attacking the *Enterprise,* he had violated the Organian Peace Treaty. The Klingon High Command officially disavowed responsibility for his actions. He was branded an outlaw, acting on his own.

Unofficially, of course, it was quite a different story. The High Command would have no regrets if Korol was to rid them of the troublesome Kirk. The sensor-penetrating device on his ship was a one-of-a-kind prototype. If it continued to work successfully, it would be incorporated into all Klingon warships. It was an interesting field test.

The blood oath was Korol's business, a matter of honor. It was between himself, his priest, and Kirk.

Korol paced the control room, deep in thought. There were many puzzling aspects to the situation. He didn't like them at all.

Foremost in his mind was why the *Enterprise* had made no response to his attack. They hadn't fired a single phaser. Nor had they turned tail and run. They just sat there and took everything the ship threw at them. It didn't make any sense. They could only lose that way.

It wasn't normal behavior for a Federation crew, and that made him wary. He wanted to proceed slowly, deliberately. He was close to his quarry—very close— but he smelled a trap. That was the only explanation that made any sense.

Why else would they just sit there? Why else would they be there in the first place?

There was another confusing aspect. When they had intercepted the subspace communication from the planet there had been no mention of Federation ships. It had simply been a diplomatic request, and he had been the nearest ship. Although he was technically an outlaw, unable to speak for the Klingon Empire, that was just a minor point. One that could be glossed over, for sure, if they claimed control of a planet over the Federation.

But why was the *Enterprise* here? There were too many loose ends.

"Lord, there is still no offensive action from the Federation ship. Should I—"

"You should follow orders," said Korol sharply, cutting off his first officer's words. "Maintain random firing pattern until I say differently."

"Yes, Lord."

"I am going to my quarters. Send the priest to me."

"Yes, Lord."

Korol's quarters were spartan, but functional. As commander, he could have whatever he wanted. As a Klingon, he wanted nothing more than was necessary. A desk, a chair, a hard bed. The frills were for people who were soft, either in the heart or the head. He professed to neither of these deficiencies. Knocking discreetly, the priest entered.

"You sent for me, Korol?"

"Sit down, priest, and listen. I sent for you because that dog of a first officer has dried mako for brains. The science officer is not doing much better. They have no answers, they don't listen well. Perhaps you will listen. Besides . . ." His voice trailed off.

"It concerns your blood oath. Am I correct, Korol?"

"You talk too much, Kirl, priest of my father. If it weren't for your age, I would not tolerate that on my ship."

"Your father tolerated it. And your brother—may he fight battles in the everlasting—tolerated it. I am an old man, but yet I have my senses and the wisdom of my age."

"Your age, hah. The days when you lifted sword against your enemies have long passed, Kirl."

"But my mind is not yet dull, Korol."

"So tell me what you think, priest. About the position we find ourselves in."

"You want the man Kirk, don't you?"

"Of course, feeble one. The oath."

75

"Is he on the ship or on the planet?"

"I have reason to believe he is on the planet's surface, the dog who should not live."

"So it is plain. You should go there and kill him."

"Hah! How little you know. I smell a trap."

"And I have lived longer than you, son of your father, and I see no trap."

"Then it will harm nothing to destroy the ship and then get Kirk."

"Do I detect cowardice?"

"Do I detect insubordination, priest? Or disrespect? Need I remind you I hold the power of life or death above you and the rest of the crew?"

"I have faced death many times, Korol. It no longer frightens me."

"Old man," muttered Korol, turning his back to the priest, facing the wall, hands clasped behind his back. "I give them one hour," he said quietly. "If there is no change in their posture by then, I shall mount an all-out attack. It will give Kirk much pain to see his ship destroyed. Then I shall go to the surface and kill him. By my hand he shall die."

"If such is your will," said Kirl evenly.

"I detect a note of disapproval," said Korol, turning.

"No, Commander. I have lived too long to make a mistake such as that. If it is your will, so be it."

"You are dismissed, priest," said Korol sharply.

The priest rose, raised a fist. "Survive and succeed," he said, bitterness in his voice.

Korol gave a nod, watched the old man leave. Fool. It was not good to grow old like that. Better to die young, on the field of battle. It would be a long hour. He rubbed his hands together. He could hardly wait.

"Are you sure you know what you're doing, Spock?" asked McCoy. "We could go on forever like this."

Spock gave McCoy a pained expression. "We are near an end of one of the underground corridors, Doctor. It is logical to assume there must be an entrance nearby."

"Still, I don't—"

Spock froze. It was so sudden that McCoy stopped short. He and Kirk followed Spock's gaze across the street. There wasn't much to see—a few people, a little movement.

"I saw one," he said quietly.

"Where?" asked Kirk.

"He entered that building," said Spock, pointing toward a nondescript general store. They rushed across the street.

"May I help you?" asked the storekeeper as they entered the small shop.

"A man just came in here," said Kirk. "Where is he?"

"You can see I am alone," said the man. "There have been no customers for several minutes."

Spock shook his head. "I saw him."

"Where is he?" asked Kirk again, sharper this time.

"I'm alone, citizen. You can see that. Bless peace, I know nothing of anyone else."

"He's probably telling the truth, Captain," said Spock. "At least the truth as he perceives it. Still, the man came in here."

"Look!" yelled McCoy from the back of the store. "I think I've found something."

Spock and Kirk joined him. Behind a counter, half hidden by a rug was a large loose tile. A person could easily squeeze through the space.

"What do you think?" asked McCoy.

"I think our man went down here," said Kirk. Dropping to his knees, he slid the rug and tile aside. Below was a drop of about three meters into a dimly lit passageway.

"That's our tunnel," said McCoy.

Kirk nodded. "Let's go," he said, lowering himself through the hole.

The drop wasn't bad and after their eyes had grown accustomed to the dim light, they realized they were at one of the ends of a tunnel.

"That makes it easy," said Kirk. "Only one way to go."

"Before we start, Captain," said Spock, "I'd like to take a few readings."

He swung the tricorder from his shoulder and made a few adjustments.

"Just as I thought, Captain. I can get readings within the tunnel network, but it won't penetrate to the outside. These walls are well shielded. I'm getting a clear indication of computer activity as well as several sources of human life."

"I don't suppose the communicators work," said Kirk.

"I doubt it," said Spock.

Kirk tried it anyway. "Kirk to *Enterprise*." There was no answer, only the faint buzz of static. "I didn't really expect anything," he said and started to close it.

"Captain!" It was Uhura's voice—over the communicator.

"Uhura. Where are you?"

"Be careful, Captain. They'll—" The transmission broke off abruptly.

"Uhura. *Uhura!* Come in." Nothing.

"That transmission came from within the tunnel network, Captain," said Spock. "I have taken a preliminary reading with the tricorder. We should be able to find her."

"Lead on," said Kirk and they headed down the tunnel.

It wasn't as easy as Spock had made it seem. The tunnel twisted and turned, branched off continuously. They made several wrong turns, had to backtrack often. Uhura's communicator was obviously broken, but it sent off a faint, erratic signal. They used it as a homing device, tracking it with the tricorder. Slowly they made their way toward the signal.

At one junction Spock paused.

"Captain," he said. "I'm getting a rapid increase in computer activity. It's quite close."

"Close enough," said a voice from behind them.

As they whirled around, they were facing Wayne Perry. He had a phaser in his hand.

"You will go no further," he said.

CHAPTER TEN

Kirk found his voice. "Okay, Wayne Perry, whoever or whatever you are, you're through pushing us around."

Perry laughed. "You're hardly in a position to make demands."

Kirk took a step toward Perry, staggered. Spock caught him before he fell.

"I don't believe the phaser is necessary," said Spock.

"An interesting toy, isn't it? I'll hold on to it for a while. It may come in handy."

"I don't doubt you are capable of using it," said Spock, "but it seems unnecessary. It is certainly illogical for one who preaches nonviolence to carry one about. I am quite disappointed."

"Disappointed?"

"Computers are presumably logical."

"Ah, you know my little secret."

"Hardly a secret," said Kirk, straightening up. "We've known it from the start. The only question is why."

"I suppose I do owe you an explanation of sorts, especially for the Vulcan. His logic appeals to the computer half of me."

"Half?" asked McCoy.

"It started about twenty years after we left Earth on the *Marilee*. I was on alternate deep sleep and slowdown. I had planned to see the ship safely to its destination, this planet. However, the wake cycles became increasingly painful to me. I consulted the medical analyzer and discovered I had Dexter's disease. It was a terminal case, inoperable, untreatable. It was only a matter of time. Yet the ship depended on me, they would need me on the voyage and upon settling on the planet. There was no one I could train who could carry on for me. It was *necessary* for me to live, if not for myself, then for the others. They deserved me, they needed me. They could not survive without me. So I did the only logical thing."

"Logical?" asked Spock, raising an eyebrow.

"Before I amassed the wealth to begin the voyage, I had been trained in biorobotics. It is, I presume, a dead science now, but at the time it dealt with androids and such. I was also an artist of sorts. My holograms were exhibited throughout the world. I created the construct you now see before you. It was meant to guide the people to the planet, to give them confidence to go on. The plan was that they would accept the construct as the real person. It served its purpose admirably."

"Fascinating," said Spock. McCoy and Kirk glared at him.

"It was only after we had reached this planet that I realized the real work still lay before us. It was not logical that I just disappear, or turn myself off, just when I was so needed. The first two winters were hard. We stripped the ship and constructed the tunnel network. It protected us from the elements. Only later did we gradually start building on the surface. We were a tightly knit society and I, as captain, was in charge."

"That must have been quite a while ago," said McCoy.

Perry nodded. "Almost three hundred years. It hasn't seemed that long. When the original colonists started to die off it caught me by surprise. I hadn't realized so much time had passed. But there were children, lots of them, and they looked upon me as their leader as naturally as their parents had. There was every reason to continue as before, even more reason."

"Oh?" said Spock. "Why was that?"

"It became apparent to me that I had an ideal situation in which to build a perfect society. We were isolated, yet had a firm hold on the planet. We had a fair technology and good equipment. After all, we had come prepared to deal with a much harsher world. So over the years I directed the society inward—in the direction of peace and tranquillity. By the very nature of our closed system, we had no enemies and peace came quickly."

"Not without a little help from you, I'm sure," said Kirk.

"It wasn't easy at first. There were malcontents, loners, people who couldn't see our manifest destiny. They were dealt with, but it pained me to use violence to get rid of violence. There had to be a better way. I had time to look for it, lots of time. After several generations of research, I perfected it."

"You mean the virus," said McCoy.

"I call it the *peacekeeper* virus. It's highly effective. It's airborne and takes effect almost immediately. When it enters a person's body, it goes directly to their nervous system. It's a perfect mimic—once established there is no sign that it's there. No sign, that is, except for its effect. When a certain set of chemical conditions are met—the chemical conditions preceding rage or acts of violence—the virus swings into action, shutting the body down. After a short period of time, the person will adjust to the virus and avoid the actions that will trigger it. In effect, they become nonviolent. Totally."

"They become ciphers, less than human," said Kirk.

"I hardly think so. If anything, they become more

82

than human. They are no longer bound to the violent acts that have, for so long, held humanity back. Of course, even given that set of circumstances, there was still a lot of work to be done. You have to realize I have had a lot of time to work on this and that I am in total control of this planet. I oversee everything. It is for their betterment. I control the education of the children. They learn only one way of life—the right way."

"And that's what you're trying to export," said McCoy.

"I see a glorious era ahead. Peace shall reign throughout the universe. No longer will people war against people, take up swords against their brothers and sisters. It will be a time of peace, a time of great advances."

"It will be a time of chaos," said Kirk.

"I seriously doubt that. Oh, I expect there will be resistance at first from people who cannot see the blessings it will bring. Violence has for too long been accepted as a necessary part of life. It will take time for people to realize that it is simply not true, but they too will come around."

"You have taken away the ability of people to defend themselves," said Kirk bitterly. "At this very moment my ship is helpless against an aggressor. Tell me how this leads to peace."

"That is simply a temporary condition. I never said that there would be no casualties. Your ship is merely one of the first. It is a small factor, really, in the larger scheme of things. A small price to pay for universal peace."

"Hardly universal," said Spock.

"What do you mean?"

"Here on your own planet there are people who are unaffected by the virus."

"That—that is simply a temporary setback. They

are few in number, and mostly sterile. They are dying out. It is of no consequence."

"Wrong," said Spock. "If there exist people who are unaffected by the virus it is logical to assume that, given the scope of the universe, others will turn up. Perhaps there will be entire races of people who are immune to the virus. The sheer weight of numbers of planets and races in the universe would make this event highly probable. To be successful, even on your terms, the virus would have to be one hundred percent effective. By your own admission, it is not. Therefore your experiment must be considered a failure."

"*No!*" shouted Perry, visible shaken. "I cannot accept that line of reasoning. The Immunes are a temporary phenomenon, transient. They will not last. Soon they will all be dead."

"That, however, will not erase the probability of it happening again," said Spock.

"It will *not* happen again," said Perry. "It cannot happen. It was a fluke."

"It was inevitable," said Spock. "The probability of it not occurring was infinitesimal."

"That's not true."

"It *is* true," said Spock. "And furthermore, for a computer, you are highly illogical."

"And for a Vulcan, you—" Perry stopped short, he cocked his head, listening for something. A wave of fear came over his face and he turned abruptly, headed down a corridor.

"What was—"

Spock shushed McCoy. "Someone's coming. Two men by their voices."

"I don't hear anything," said McCoy.

"I do," said Spock. "I believe it would be prudent to leave at this point."

They rushed down a branching corridor away from the voices, trying to keep as quiet as possible. It was a corridor picked at random. It was a wrong choice. A dead end. Even McCoy could hear the voices now. They were getting closer.

"Gentlemen," Spock whispered, "I believe we're about to meet the Immunes."

CHAPTER ELEVEN

The bridge of the *Enterprise* was bathed in the dim red light of the emergency power. Everything else was being shunted to maintain the shields. Almost all the systems aboard were in their maximum power-down mode to conserve what they had left. It might give them a few more minutes. Scotty shook his head, thumbed the intercom open.

"Bridge to Engineerin'."

"Nason here, sir."

"How much time ha'e we left?" How often had he asked that question? The numbers kept getting smaller.

"I make it thirty minutes, sir."

"That's all? Are you sure, mon?"

"No, I'm not sure. It could be twenty minutes. The decay is growing more pronounced."

"Carry on. Bridge out."

Chekov was livid. "Carry on? How can you say that at a time like this?"

"An' what would you expect me to say, Mister Chekov? Do you have a magic rabbit to pull out of your Rooshian hat? Of course we carry on. We always have and we always will."

"I don't like it."

"None of us like it, Mister Chekov, but there is very little we can do about it. Giving up will not help matters at all."

"I wasn't giving up. It just seems that there ought to be something we could do."

86

"If ye think o' somethin', be sure and let me know."

Scotty regretted being so sharp with the boy, but everyone was on edge. Losing contact with Kirk and the crew on Perry hadn't helped. It had only increased their own feelings of isolation and helplessness. Scotty assumed the loss of communication meant that they had, as planned, worked their way into the underground network of tunnels. Maybe they would find something that could help, though there wasn't much time left. Even Spock had failed to come up with any suggestions before they lost contact. That was terribly disappointing to Scotty. He had been counting on the Vulcan's keen mind to come up with something. It wasn't like Spock to let them down. That made the situation seem even more hopeless.

"Excuse me, sir," said Sulu. "Our orbit is starting to slip. Should I correct for it?"

"How serious is it?"

"Not very. It shouldn't amount to much for another hour or so."

By then it won't matter, thought Scotty. "Ignore it for now," he said. "We need the power for the shields."

"Yes, sir."

We need more than that, thought Scotty. We need a plan, any plan. We need a miracle. Even a little one would do.

The hour was almost up. Korol was staying in his quarters until the last minute. He practically had Kirk in the palm of his hand.

High Command would be pleased at the loss of the *Enterprise* and her captain, long a thorn in the side of Klingons everywhere. Once again they would disavow Korol's actions. A blood oath was a personal thing, beyond the control of the state.

On the other hand, perhaps they might not. After all, treaties were made to be broken when the time was right. The time certainly seemed right.

One of the keys to the matter was the sensor-pene-trating device. It was a simple machine based on a previously undetected flaw in the Federation sensor system. If the Federation was to get their hands on one of the machines, it would be easy for them to determine how it worked and to correct the original flaw. Therefore, the matter became urgent. If it was to be used it would have to be used soon and on a massive scale. The treaty would have to be broken and the Federation fleet totally wiped out. So far the machine had worked perfectly. Conquest of the entire Federation seemed within their grasp.

Only a few minutes left. Korol still suspected a trap, but once committed to a plan of action, his feelings of indecision had left him. Surely if the *Enterprise* wasn't as helpless as it looked it would have done something by now. If it didn't put up a fight, it would be destroyed. It was that simple. The loss of the ship would make Kirk particularly vulnerable.

It would be good to avenge his brother. The knot of hate in his belly would ease a bit.

He watched the digital on his wall tick off another minute. He would be punctual.

And deadly.

Kirk opened his eyes and tried to focus. The first thing he saw was Spock.

"How long have I been out?" he asked.

"Not long, Captain. You tried to resist when the Immunes found us, and it triggered the virus. You passed out, as did Dr. McCoy. I found it illogical, under the conditions, to resist. They handled both of you quite roughly, but I was unable to come to your assistance."

"McCoy. Is he—"

"He seems to be fully recovered. At present he is tending to Lieutenant Uhura and Dr. Davis. They fared rather less well than we did."

"Where are they?" asked Kirk, sitting up, looking around. McCoy was across the room, bent over the supine forms of Uhura and Kelly Davis. "Bones," he called out.

"They're okay, Jim," said McCoy. "Considering the circumstances."

Spock helped Kirk to his feet. They crossed the room. It was dark, dirty, with a door of heavy iron bars. A guard was sitting outside. They joined McCoy. Uhura looked terrible, Kelly Davis only slightly better. Kirk felt rage rising. He suppressed it with difficulty.

"What happened?" he asked.

"They were kidnapped," said McCoy. "Though perhaps for different reasons than we were." There was bitterness in his voice.

"Perhaps I should explain," said Spock.

"I wish somebody would," said Kirk.

"While you were unconscious I had occasion to converse with the guard. He, like all the other Immunes, is quite unintelligent, but I managed to gather some information."

Kelly Davis sat up, rubbed the side of her face. Her jaw was swollen. "I've talked to them, too. At least when they weren't knocking me around."

"Good," said Spock. "By combining our impressions, we might be able to produce a clear picture of these people."

"Why does everybody know what's happening but me?" asked Kirk.

"Because you have been unconscious, Captain," said Spock as if it were the most obvious thing in the world.

"Then I suppose you wouldn't mind filling me in, Mr. Spock," said Kirk with a heavy layer of sarcasm in his voice.

"Of course not. The Immunes are subnormal mentally only partly because they exist outside the mainstream of society on Perry, without the somewhat questionable benefit of Captain Perry's guided educational program. Far more important is the fact that they have never *had* to learn anything. If they need something, they take it. If someone gets in their way, they knock him down. It's as simple as that."

"They're never opposed," said Kelly. "The virus and subsequent conditioning of the people on this planet make it quite impossible for them to resist. In fact, most of them are incapable of even noticing the Immunes."

"They block them out," said Spock. "The shopkeeper was telling the truth when he said he hadn't seen the man enter. The Immunes, like violence, are blind spots to most of the people on this planet, the so-called normal people."

"It's a genetic trait," said McCoy. "Something in their metabolism makes them immune to the virus action. Given time and the proper equipment, we could probably isolate the substance, create a cofactor against the virus to neutralize its effect."

"Time is something we're short of right now," said Kirk.

"One more thing, Jim. Perry was right about the Immunes being mostly sterile. They—they mate with the normals whenever possible."

It took a moment for that to sink in. He looked at the bruised and battered Uhura and Kelly Davis. "Did they—"

"Easy, Jim. Nothing so far—but like you said, we're running out of time. In more ways than one."

Kirk turned. "Spock. What about the computer?"

"Two things, one a fact and one a conjecture. First, I believe I have determined the location of the master computer. As we were being brought to this cell I took advantage of the time to take some detailed tricorder readings. There is an area of intense computer activity not far from here. Most likely it is the source we are looking for."

"I assume that's the fact, Mr. Spock."

"Of course, Captain."

"And the conjecture?"

"I am not convinced that Wayne Perry is wholly a computer construct."

"What?" asked Kirk. "What do you mean by that?"

"I thought you said Wayne Perry wasn't alive," said McCoy. "Can't you make up your mind?"

"The facts haven't changed, Doctor. The object you perceive *is* a construct. It is composed of metal, wires, and crystals, given its shape by a highly sophisticated holographic projection. It is no more alive than these walls."

"So?" asked Kirk.

"I first detected something wrong when Wayne Perry exhibited such illogical thoughts about the Immunes and the so-called peacekeeping virus. It was not only irrational on the subject, it was inconsistent in its reasoning. Such behavior is highly unbecoming in a computer, even a faultily programmed one. Since we can assume the original Wayne Perry was reasonably intelligent, its initial programming was probably sufficient. Therefore, the original programming is being modified in some way. The most probable source of modification would be an interface with a living system."

"You mean someone is changing the program as the years go by?" asked Kirk.

"Perhaps," said Spock. "There is also the fact that the construct left as the Immunes were approaching, even though it carried a phaser and presumably would have been able to use it. It was obviously afraid of them, though it had no reason to be. This is illogical. Its behavior is more typical of a human than a computer."

"Are you trying to be funny, Spock?" asked McCoy.

"I was simply stating a fact, Doctor. I would like to meet Wayne Perry again to explore this further."

"We're not going to get anywhere if we don't—" Kirk was cut off as the cell door swung open. The guard walked in with the easy, confident gait of someone who has never been seriously opposed in his life. He looked casually at his prisoners, settled on Uhura.

"I take," he said.

Uhura shrank back. Kelly Davis moved to protect her, though it was useless. He could do what he wanted, take whatever he wished.

McCoy reached over and pulled the tricorder from Spock's shoulder, approached the Immune.

"You're a sick man," he said, waving the tricorder at him.

"Me sick?"

The tricorder split the air with a piercing wail. The Immune took a careful step backward. Spock realized that McCoy had adjusted the tricorder so that it would monitor the man's heartbeat. He had switched to audio and turned the gain way up. The resulting screeching feedback was most impressive.

"I'm a doctor and this says you're a sick man, very sick." He pointed at the man's left arm. It was half covered by an ugly sore, obviously infected. "I can fix that for you."

"Fix?"

McCoy took a step toward him. "I'll bet that hurts."

The man touched his arm. "It hurts. Yes."

"I can make it stop hurting."

The man looked at him suspiciously. "You not Green."

"I wear no scarf, like you," said McCoy. "But like the Greens, I heal."

The man pushed his arm toward McCoy. He had nothing to fear. "You fix."

McCoy took the spray hypo from the medikit on his utility belt and poised it over the man's arm. It hissed and the man slowly slumped to the floor. McCoy eased him down to make sure he wasn't injured.

"Let's go," said Kirk, helping Uhura to her feet.

McCoy frowned, shook his head. "Wait," he said, removing the spray applicator from his medikit. Slowly, and with great care he covered the wound with an antibiotic.

"I had to do that, Jim," he said, replacing his equipment. "It's in my nature to heal. He was suffering. Treating that might have stung him a little if he'd been awake. Since, thanks to the virus, I'm incapable of hurting anyone . . ."

"So you had to put him to sleep," said Kirk.

"He'll be out about an hour," smiled McCoy. "I also managed to collect a small tissue sample. When we get back to the *Enterprise* we should have no trouble generating the cofactor."

"Very interesting, Doctor," said Spock. "But what if there is no *Enterprise?*" There was no answer to that question. Spock had already calculated that the ship ought to be running out of power any minute. He kept that information to himself.

"Now let's go," said Kirk. This time no one objected.

The digital on Korol's wall ticked off another minute, the last one. He smiled with satisfaction, palmed the intercom open.

"Korol here. Bring the phasers to full power. I'm on my way to the bridge."

"Yes, Lord."

Korol broke the connection, rose from his chair. So this is how the *Enterprise* ends, he thought. And the Captain next. He grinned as he left his room.

His grin was one of pure evil.

CHAPTER TWELVE

Scotty never imagined the end would come this way. He had always figured if they went out, they'd go out fighting. Not this way; not without Kirk at the helm, not without so much as a phaser burst.

The sitting, the waiting, watching helplessly as the minutes slowly ticked off one by one. Each minute gone forever.

"Sir, there must be something . . ." said Sulu, his voice trailing off as he realized he'd said this before. Many times. He was just talking to hear the sound of his own voice. "Sorry," he said.

"That's all right, Mr. Sulu," said Scotty. "I know what you mean. We'll just keep tryin' to reach the Captain and hope the situation will change. That's about all we can do."

"I can't take this!" shouted Chekov, rising from his chair on the command module. "We can't just sit here like this."

"Easy, mon," said Scotty. "If there was somethin' to do, we'd be doin' it."

"Can't we—can't we—" His voice faded out.

"Do you want to be relieved, Mr. Chekov?" asked Scotty quietly.

Chekov stood for a moment, muscles tense. He thought of his heritage, of the thousands before him that had gone down with their ships. He sat back down.

"No, sir," he said in a hushed voice. "I'll see this through."

"Good mon," said Scotty.

With a sigh, he placed another call to Engineering.

"Nason here, sir. About five minutes, maybe four. The readings are getting fuzzy at the low end. We've *got* to drop the shields."

"That's impossible," said Scotty.

"If we don't drop the shields, we're dead. The crystals will go out on the flat end and they'll never come back. If we drop the shields we can slowly build them back up."

"I know that, Mr. Nason, but it doesn't help at all. If we drop the shields we're dead, too. The Klingons will see to that."

"In about four minutes it will be a moot point. We might as well give up hope."

"Mr. Nason—we will never give up hope, never. We . . ."

"Mr. Scott?"

Something tugged at the edge of Scotty's mind, an elusive thought, the germ of an idea. If only Mr. Spock were here.

"Mr. Scott?"

It might work, it might not. Better to try something and fail than to do nothing at all. It was a long shot, the odds were all against it, but still . . .

"Mr. Scott, are you there?"

Anything was worth trying at this point.

"Aye, lad. Meet me in the transporter room on the double."

"The transporter room?"

"Move!" Scotty bolted from his chair. "Wish me luck, men," he said as he headed for the door.

"Luck?" said Sulu. "What—"

"No time to explain," said Scotty, leaving the bridge in a rush.

Sulu and Chekov looked at each other. What could all this mean? Had Scotty taken leave of his senses? There was only one thing to do and that was to carry on. To the bitter end. Another call was placed to the planet's surface.

As usual, there was no answer.

Spock cut around the corner, hugged the wall. Seeing that the corridor was deserted, he motioned for Kirk to follow. In the dim light, the two men made their way deeper and deeper into the maze of corridors.

When they had left the cell, they decided that the best thing to do would be to split up into two groups. McCoy, Uhura, and Kelly Davis were, with any luck, making their way to the surface. Once there, it was hoped they would be able to contact the ship, get beamed aboard and start work on a cure for the virus. Of course, that depended on a lot of factors, mostly unpredictable—like a safe passage to the surface and the survival of the ship. Spock reckoned both of these to have a very low probability at this point.

It wasn't too far from the cell to the nexus of computer activity that Spock had discovered, but there was no direct way there. The corridors twisted and branched with distressing frequency. Their route was made even more difficult by the occasional Immune roaming the corridor, causing them to backtrack often, take other options.

"How much further?" whispered Kirk.

"Not far," answered Spock. "Two more turns."

They made their way down to the next intersection, walking as quietly as they could, staying as near to the wall as possible. The corridors were dimly lit from light panels imbedded in the ceilings. Spock had noticed that the panels were organic in nature, the light being produced by colonies of phosphorescent plankton. Their dimness meant that the colonies were dying out. He supposed they had been installed back when the corridors had first been constructed, soon after the arrival of the settlers. Their dying out indicated a lack of upkeep, a carelessness in maintaining the corridors. Somehow it fit the picture of the computer construct Wayne Perry, a gradual disintegration from a once-noble ideal. The floor of the corridors was covered in places by debris. More decay.

They reached the corner, waited quietly, slipped around when they decided it was clear.

"It should be at the end of this corridor, Captain," whispered Spock.

"I don't see anything."

"It should be off to the left."

As they reached the end of the corridor, they discovered a small alcove to the left. There was one door off the alcove. It was unmarked, unremarkable in every way. It was locked.

"Are you sure this is the place?" asked Kirk. "It doesn't look like anything at all."

"When hiding something of value, Captain, it is often useful not to draw attention to it."

Kirk tried the door. It didn't move. The lock looked complicated.

"Another dead end," he said dejectedly.

"Perhaps not," said Spock, bending over to inspect the lock. "Everything I have seen down here shows a remarkable lack of sophistication. Since this was the first part of the planet they inhabited, it would stand to reason it would be the least complicated. After all, this area was never meant to be a permanent part of their city, only a temporary place to live. There have been few, if any, signs of maintenance or updating or anything down here." He fiddled with the lock a little, found a small piece of wire in the clutter against the wall, probed it for a while.

"How are you at picking locks?" asked Kirk.

"It appears to be one of my talents," said Spock, standing up, pushing the door open with one finger.

"You constantly surprise me," said Kirk.

"I should hope so. Shall we enter?"

The room was large, the walls filled with gauges, dials, and flashing lights. A huge console stood in one corner. They ignored it all. The thing that held their attention was a transparent dome in the middle of the room.

Inside the dome was a platform. On the platform lay a man. His hair was long, pure white, cascading nearly to the floor. His fingernails were at least six inches long. Wires and tubes led from his body to a control board.

"What the devil is that?" asked Kirk.

"I believe we have found the computer's interface with a living system."

"That, that . . . thing is alive?"

"Barely, Captain, just barely. He seems to be in a state just above that of suspended animation, very much like deep sleep."

They walked over to the platform. The room reminded Kirk of a mausoleum, the dome a crypt, the man a corpse.

"Look closely, Captain."

The man was old, how old it was impossible to tell. His face was a mass of wrinkles, age lines cut deep into his features, features somehow familiar. His eyes were dull, unseeing, devoid of life.

"That's Wayne Perry!" said Kirk.

Spock nodded. "The *original* Wayne Perry."

Korol stood on the bridge of the Klingon vessel, the priest behind him and to his left. He faced their viewscreen, which held the image of the *Enterprise,* a helpless ship from all appearances.

"Lord, the phaser banks are at full power."

Korol nodded, savoring the moment. It had been long in coming. He wanted it to be right.

"Two more bursts of random fire," he said. "Then let loose with everything. Keep it up until there is nothing left of that ship. I want it totally destroyed."

"That should be about sixty seconds from now, Lord," said the officer.

"Will they be able to block that attack?" asked the priest.

"No," said Korol. "There is no way they can stop it now. They're as good as dead."

Scotty was adjusting the transporter controls when Nason rushed into the room.

"Have you gone crazy?" asked Nason. "We can't use the transporter."

"We have to. Don't argue." Scotty stepped from behind the console and rushed toward the platform.

"We'll have to drop the shields. They'll blast us to pieces."

"They're goin' to blast us anyway. Either that or we're goin' to run out of power. We're dead both ways. The controls are set." He raised his voice. "Mr. Sulu. Can you hear me?"

"I can hear you, but I don't understand," he said over the open intercom.

"You don't have to understand. Just drop the shields after the next phaser burst. Drop them long enough for Nason to hit the transporter controls. Then raise them."

"Sir," said Nason. "We have only a couple of minutes left. Are you sure that—"

"Here it comes," said Sulu. "Shields down."

"Energize," said Scotty, but Nason was already moving the controls.

"That's it," said Korol. "Hit them with everything. *Fire!*"

At that instant, Scotty materialized on the bridge of the Klingon vessel. The gunnery officer was bent over the firing stud.

"*Lord!*" he shouted. "I can't do it." With a twist, he fell from his chair to the floor.

Korol stood frozen, torn between the firing stud and Scotty. He charged Scotty, but only managed three paces before he too collapsed.

Pandemonium reigned on the Klingon bridge. Everyone seemed to rush Scotty at once. Stumbling over each other, they fell to the floor.

"I surrender," said Scotty, waving his arms expansively, a huge grin on his face. More Klingons fell, some heading for him, others to the firing stud. It was obvious they could get near neither one. Scotty whipped out his communicator.

"Scott to *Enterprise*," he said.

"Sulu here, Mr. Scott. Where are you? What's happening?"

"Drop the shields, Mr. Sulu. Have Mr. Nason begin salvaging the dilithium crystals. I don't think we'll have any more trooble wi' with Klingons."

"What do you mean, Mr. Scott?"

"I'm on the Klingon bridge right now. Things seem to be quiet here. Verra peaceful, as a matter of fact."

In the background, Scotty could hear laughter from the crew of the *Enterprise*'s bridge.

It was a rare and welcome sound.

CHAPTER THIRTEEN

Rus sat inside his work cubicle in one of the back rooms of the building that housed the Council chambers. A stream of numbers flowed across the screen in front of him. Occasionally he would slow down the numbers, make a few notations on a pad. From the muted noises he could tell that Ami was working in the cubicle beside his.

Pages kept track of all sorts of Council business. It was supposed to be important work, but usually it was just boring. They waded through huge amounts of facts and figures, selecting those few that should be brought to the Council's attention. A vast amount of truly trivial information came out of the computer every day. Most of it was useless, but every now and then something of value came up. Usually it was associated with one of the Council members' current projects. Most of the day-by-day material—individual's credit levels, etc.—were handled exclusively by the master computer, only the oddball stuff came through his and Ami's terminals. Still, that was more than enough. Lately it had been throwing up more garbage than usual. Right now it was analyzing the purchasing habits of citizens between the ages of seventeen and twenty-three. It was trivial. He dozed slightly, was jarred by a small chime.

He almost missed it, a small piece of data flagged SRT. For some reason all SRTs had to be filed for

Councilman Jon. Irritated, he hit the slide-back and reversed the flow of numbers. He held the switch down too long and overshot it. Mad at himself, he snapped his stylus in two.

Immediately, he broke into a cold sweat. It was a familar feeling, one he got every time he did something associated with rage. He was sure no one had seen him, but that didn't help.

He had to hide his violent emotions. He'd had to do it all his life.

His father, the father Rus had never known, had been an Immune. He inherited the trait.

His mother, a kind, quiet person, was in every way a normal inhabitant of Perry. That is, she was totally nonviolent, with no say in the matter. She knew that if her son was discovered to have violent tendencies he would be banished or worse. Most of the upbringing that Rus had was aimed at curbing his natural impulses. It had been difficult from the beginning.

Luckily, Rus was highly intelligent. He had realized at a very early age that he had to keep his emotions under tight control. It was never easy, but, for the most part, he managed.

As a child, when he held back his temper, it usually came to the surface as tears. As an adult, it came back as frustration. Once every month or so, Rus would take to the woods, find a deserted place and scream and yell until he was hoarse. It seldom helped very much. He knew of the corridors where the Immunes dwelt. He watched the Immunes carefully, always searching for a face, the face of his unknown father.

He felt he lived in a twilight world, seeing things that neither the Immunes nor normal people could see. Most normals so totally rejected violence they were unable to even comprehend the existence of the Immunes. The Immunes, on the other hand, treated the normals as if they were furniture, mere objects to be used when the occasion arose. In many ways Rus was repulsed by both groups, in other ways he was drawn to both. It was the only world he knew and he wanted desperately to fit, but deep inside he realized he would never be able to.

He had a strong feeling that Wayne Perry, like himself, lived in two worlds. There was nothing he could identify that would confirm that, but he felt it deeply. It had drawn him to pledge the Council.

Rus tagged the SRT for Councilman Jon. The screen started up again. He swallowed his temper, as he had done so many times before. He could not afford to make mistakes.

Spock finished his tricorder readings. "There is no doubt in my mind that this is the original Wayne Perry," he said.

"But how? And why? It doesn't make any sense."

"It makes a warped kind of sense when you consider the effects of Dexter's disease."

"What's that?"

"I should have realized it before," said Spock. "The construct said that Wayne Perry was suffering from Dexter's disease. One of the effects is mental degeneration, usually characterized by megalomania."

"Megalomania?"

"Delusions of grandeur, an obsession with doing extravagant things. That would explain his blindness to the obvious faults in his master plan for this planet and, indeed, the universe."

"Why the body?" asked Kirk.

"Two reasons. An interface with a human being would give the computer more flexibility. It could change and adapt as the situation shifted. Of course it has the disadvantage of introducing the human's subjective and irrational thought processes into the computer. It makes for a very sloppy computer."

"The second reason?"

"I suspect that at one time Wayne Perry wanted immortality. To live forever would give him time to fulfill his grand plan, to see it through to fruition. It would fit with the pattern of megalomania, though I doubt that—given a chance to freely express himself— he would desire it now."

"Why is that?"

"This body is in great pain. It has been in pain for hundreds of years, unable to do anything about it. The level of life in this body is so low that I doubt it has been aware of anything *but* pain for the last two hundred years. It is bound to have had an effect on the computer and its construct."

"All those years of pain," muttered Kirk. "It must be intolerable."

"The most humane thing to do would be to end his suffering, though of course we are incapable of it."

"Isn't there anything we can do?"

"For Wayne Perry, no. For us, yes. Somewhere in this computer is the answer to the virus. If we can gain access to that information it should enable us to improve our currently untenable position."

"Where do we start?" asked Kirk.

Spock was already walking to what appeared to be an access panel. He looked at it and frowned. "This may take some time," he said, bending over the keyboard.

Kirk paced the room. "This is a crazy planet," he muttered. "Crazy people, a crazy computer ruling it."

"It's a dying planet," said Spock, not looking up from the computer.

"How's that?"

"One need only look around, Captain, to see signs of decay. This colony could have flourished on this planet, but it is headed, thanks to Wayne Perry, toward a dead end. The Immunes could crush this society if they had the inclination. The citizens would do much better without the supposed guidance of their benefactor. They are on a downhill slide."

"Let's hope they don't take us with them."

"Good point, Captain. I'm working on that."

"Any luck?"

"Like many things on this planet, the computer seems complex on the surface, but actually is quite simple. The interface with the body of Wayne Perry is the only complication. It muddles the readings, throws up barriers. There is a strong urge for self-preservation encoded into the system. I assume it started with Wayne Perry and has been increased and maintained by the computer."

"The virus?"

"It shouldn't take long now. I'm getting to it."

"I think not." It was Wayne Perry's voice. Or, rather, the voice of the Wayne Perry construct.

Both men whirled around. The construct was standing in the doorway.

"I'm sorry you got this far," it said. "It will grieve me to kill you."

Working. Dilithium crystals are currently at 0.02% of normal functioning levels. Revitalization procedures presently in effect will produce an initial rise of 0.05% efficiency per hour for the next six hours. Passing threshold levels at that time, the rise will increase— barring any unusual drain—exponentially until a peak efficiency of 0.625% of normal levels is achieved. The crystals are too depleted to come back any further than that. It is a sufficient level to achieve warp factor four and maintain it for an indefinite period of time.

"What does that mean?" asked Chekov.

"I'm not sure," said Sulu.

"Did it answer our question?"

"I don't know. Computer, how long will it be before we can use the transporter again?"

Working. Twenty-one point three minutes. If that is the answer to your previous question, then it was phrased incorrectly.

"Thanks a lot."

You are welcome.

"Endit," said Sulu.

Scotty had discovered a new dance step. He called it the Klingon two-step. Two steps and you fall down. It seemed to be quite popular on the enemy ship.

Actually, it was inherent in the Klingons. So conditioned were they to violence that it was nearly impossible for them to function without it. Especially with a human on board.

"Kind of gets to yer, disna' it," asked Scotty.

Korol could only glare at the intruder.

"Never in my life have a' seen a more peaceful group of Klingons. It warms the cockles of my heart."

"What have you done to us?" hissed Korol.

"Why, I've made you better company, of course, fit to associate with us finer folk."

"I could kill you," said Korol.

"No you couldn't," said Scotty, grinning. "And that's the whole point."

"It *was* a trap."

"Sure, it may ha'e been a trap, Commander, but it wasna' us who set it. Much as I'd like to, I canna' claim responsibility."

"Who, then?"

"Compliments of a certain Mr. Wayne Perry and the people of his most hospitable planet."

"Dogs," spat Korol.

"For once I have to agree with you. I must admit, however, that this has all turned out better than I expected."

"I should have killed you immediately."

"Correct, Commander Korol. But since you didn't, I have one more job to do."

"And what would that be?"

"You ha'e a certain piece of equipment on board that I'm verra sure the Federation would like to get its hands on. I'm speakin' o' the device you used to evade our sensors."

"You can't! I won't allow it."

Scotty's grin grew wider still. "And I suppose you're goin' to stop me?"

"I—I—" He blinked twice, caught his breath in large gasps. "Damn you, anyway," he said.

Scotty only laughed.

McCoy watched the shadowy figure go down the corridor, turn left and disappear. Was that a flash of light? He nodded at Kelly Davis, who was helping Uhura along. They followed the path of the man at a discreet distance, hoping he would lead them to an exit.

At first they had tried to follow Spock's directions back to the entrance, but that had turned out to be impossible. There were too many twists and turns, too many branching corridors, too many Immunes to avoid at all costs. McCoy was disoriented, totally lost. The corridors all looked the same to him. It wouldn't surprise him if they found themselves back at the cell when they turned the next corner.

But it wasn't the cell around the corner, just another corridor; no different, McCoy thought, than any of the others. Nothing to do but keep going.

"Wait," whispered Uhura. "Look. There."

He would have missed it, passed it by. A thin line of light in the low ceiling. It was barely visible. He stood on the tips of his toes and felt around the crack. Something moved, the crack grew wider.

"It's a panel," he said, pushing harder.

Soon he had worked the panel loose and slid it far enough to one side so that a person could squeeze through. Sunlight streamed through the opening. He lifted Kelly Davis up, then Uhura. With their help, he pulled himself through the hole into the fresh air.

They found themselves in an overgrown courtyard behind a low brick building. The sunlight nearly blinded them after so long in the dim underground. McCoy whipped out his communicator.

"McCoy to *Enterprise*." This was it. Was it still there? An instant passed. It seemed like hours. Had the ship been destroyed? Had it left?

"Dr. McCoy. Is that you?" Sulu's voice cracked. It wasn't the regulation hailing response, but nobody cared. Smiles broke out all around. The ship was safe!

"Can you beam the three of us aboard, Mr. Sulu?"

"Yes, sir, right away."

"The Klingons . . . ?"

"Mr. Scott is having a chat with them now. They seem to have become quite civilized."

"I don't understand," said McCoy. A few minutes later he did understand, but by then he was safely aboard the *Enterprise*.

The numbers on his screen stopped suddenly, faded out. When they came back, they were gibberish, they made no sense at all. Rus pushed the *clear* button, started the flow all over again. Still it was nonsense, an unconnected stream of jumbled numbers and letters. Something was wrong. He knew at this point he should send for a computer expert, but he was curious. He'd never been cured of being curious, either.

He initiated a search backward through the computer system to trace the source of the trouble. As he peeled back each layer of the computer he kept finding nothing but garbage. Eventually, he got down to the core. Still nonsense. He shut down his screen and leaned back in thought.

Something was wrong at a very basic level. That could only point to Wayne Perry. Maybe this was the chance he had been waiting for, the chance to see the two sides of the man. He knew the computer complex was located underground. Rus had explored the underground system thoroughly, he thought he had a fairly good idea where it was. He slipped out of the room silently.

He didn't notice Ami following him.

"This is not rational behavior," said Spock. "I would have expected better of you."

"I am the one who decides what behavior is rational on this planet," said the Wayne Perry construct. "I am the authority here, my word is law."

"Your authority is slipping," said Kirk. "Your empire is crumbling even as that body is decaying."

"No," said the construct. "This planet is flourishing. Peace is everywhere. I . . . the body . . . will live forever."

"The Immunes are everywhere," said Spock. "You can't ignore them."

"They will go away. They are dying out."

"Others will take their place," said Kirk.

"I will deal with them. I have always dealt with them. They are weak compared to the power of peace."

"Peace," said Spock. "An amicable goal. You cannot have peace without strength as long as there exist people who choose to impose their lives upon yours. I don't question your motives, only your procedures. I doubt this was Wayne Perry's initial intention."

"You know nothing," said the construct.

"Actually, we know quite a bit," said Spock, indicating the near-lifeless body of Wayne Perry. "An ingenious attempt, but one doomed to failure."

"It shall not fail. I am sure of that."

"The body of Wayne Perry is dying. It has been dying for many years. The interface is faulty."

"He lives through me. Through me Wayne Perry will live forever."

"Even now he dies."

"No. There is pain, to be sure, but pain can—and *must*—be endured. Below the pain is the lifeline, the brain impulses that are Wayne Perry, that are me. He lives through me."

"Do you shunt the pain?" asked Spock.

"What?" asked the construct.

"It should not be too difficult to shunt or filter the pain prior to its entrance into the computer network."

"*Spock!*" shouted Kirk.

"An intriguing idea," said the construct.

"That should let the necessary trickle of residual thought processes through, uncluttered by pain."

"Spock," said Kirk. "The body would still feel it. It would die a little more each day. What are you doing?"

"Buying us time, Captain. I'm sure the construct realizes that."

"Quite sensible of you," it said. "As a matter of fact, I have come to appreciate your logical nature. My computer half quite admires it. I think you could be of considerable use to me."

"Really?" asked Spock. "In what way?"

"I could interface you in parallel with the system just as the body of Wayne Perry is interfaced. You could never move again, but you would, in this fashion, live forever."

"An interesting possibility," said Spock, raising a quizzical eyebrow. "It would be an unusual experience, well worth experimenting with if it weren't quite so permanent. As it is, I must decline."

"You have no choice."

"You control my body, but not my mind," said Spock.

"If you choose to be uncooperative, I will kill the Captain now."

His phaser was pointed at Kirk's belly. It wasn't set on stun.

"It seems you are right," said Spock. "I have no choice."

CHAPTER FOURTEEN

Ship's Log, Lieutenant Commander Scott Recording, Stardate 6846.1:

The Klingons are in a state of utter confusion. Infected by the same virus that we carry, they are incapable of even the simplest action. Violence is too much a natural part of their lives. They can't let it go, and therefore can't do anything. Their Commander, Korol, seems particularly affected by it.

While infecting the Klingon ship—a most nonhostile action, I am sure—I managed to come into possession of the device they used to penetrate our sensors. It is a remarkably simple device and there should be no trouble at all evading it in the future.

We are much relieved to have Dr. McCoy, Lieutenant Uhura, and Dr. Davis back on board. It appears that they suffered badly at the hands of the people on the planet. Dr. McCoy has been hard at work since his return to develop the cofactor to counteract the virus. He has had innumerable problems. His work is not proceeding as rapidly as he would like.

We still have had no word from the Captain or Mr. Spock. It is assumed that they are still under the surface of the planet. Dr. McCoy indicated that the Captain wished a small party—specifically himself and Mr. Spock—to seek out the computer. Any more would draw undesirable attention. While I respect his wishes, there is a limit. We have not heard from him in a long time.

Meanwhile, we continue to hold our original orbit. The dilithium crystals are gradually coming back to the maximum level that could be expected.

"Your laxness has cost us dearly, Korol," said the priest.

"Who could tell?" Korol sat in the chair in his quarters. It was only slightly better than the confusion on the bridge.

"You should have killed them when you had the chance."

"That is easy for you to say, old man. Hindsight is the best sight there is."

"I seem to recall suggesting action. You wanted to wait."

"You recall too much. It is not healthy."

The priest laughed. "And what are you going to do to me? Boil me in oil? Hang me by my thumbs? You would have a hard time even slapping my wrists."

"I despise you, priest of my father."

"I assure you the feeling is mutual. Your father would not have found himself in this position, nor your brother. You are weak, Korol."

"We may yet find a cure. When we do, you will be the first item of business on my schedule."

"I doubt that a cure even exists, Korol. The Federation scientists are probably as baffled as our own scientists are. They would have taken defensive measures by now if they could."

"You don't call what they did to us a defensive measure?"

"Surrendering is hardly defensive."

"Infecting us was."

"That was purely a byproduct. A splendid maneuver on their part."

"I fail to appreciate it."

"In my time I have seen many things come and go, Korol. It gives one perspective."

"We don't need perspective," said Korol. "We need a cure."

"We need both," said the priest.

McCoy sat at the bench in the ship's biochemical laboratory. He was a most unhappy man.

"Worthless," he muttered. "Absolutely worthless."

Kelly Davis had just walked into the room. She sat on a stool behind him. "It's that bad?" she asked.

"Worse, if that's possible. I'm going to have to throw out the whole last batch of samples. Nothing there at all."

"Mr. Spock would probably mention that negative information is still information."

"It's still negative, too," snapped McCoy. He straightened up, wiped the sweat from his brow. "Sorry, Dr. Davis."

"It's Kelly, Dr. McCoy. And don't worry about it."

"Sorry, Kelly. I just can't seem to get close to this virus at all, much less the cofactor to counteract it. That virus is tricky, it's a perfect neural mimic. After it settles, as I presume it does, in the synapses, it's impossible to detect."

"What about the Immune sample?"

"It cultured well. I've got a large sample of it, but I don't know what good that's going to do me. I've analyzed it down to the last molecule, and I can't find any difference between that and a sample from someone normal who's infected. For that matter, my fancy machine here tells me that it can't find anything out of line with the values for a person who's *not* infected. A dead end."

"Not necessarily."

"How's that?"

"Your analyzer is a beautiful machine, but it's dumb."

"What do you mean?"

"It can only answer the questions you ask it. If it doesn't know what to look for, it'll never find it. The machine can't think for itself."

McCoy shook his head wearily. "It must have been nice when all they had to fool around with were test tubes and petri dishes. We rely on machinery entirely too much these days."

"Right. They can't do our thinking for us. We have to do that ourselves. *Then* we use the machines."

"That sounds good," said McCoy. "But I'm fresh out of ideas. Everything leads to the same place. Nothing. I'm almost convinced that this *is* a perfect peacekeeping virus, undetectable, unremovable, incurable."

"I don't agree. There is probably a solution, though it has eluded us so far. Even if there isn't, we can't give up. We have to keep trying." Her enthusiasm was infectious, even enough to get through McCoy's cynicism. A little bit.

"Any ideas?" he asked.

She smiled. "Suppose we start by hypothesizing a multiphasic, dipolar organism and work from there."

"That's way out in left field," said McCoy.

"We have to start somewhere," she said. "Now let's get back to the culture."

"It's worth a try."

McCoy started to clear off the bench, reprogram the analyzer.

"Dr. Davis," he said. "You are one fine researcher."

"Kelly," she said.

"Kelly it is."

And one fine woman, too, he thought.

Spock lay on a slab just outside the transparent dome. The Wayne Perry construct was carefully inserting small wires into his scalp. The wires led to a multi-pronged plug that would be inserted into the computer.

"I'm not sure this will work," it said, bending over Spock.

"That is not especially encouraging," said Spock.

"It wasn't meant to be. I was simply stating a fact. You have a strong personality, perhaps too strong. It is possible you could cause some amount of confusion when interfaced with the computer. Therefore I am introducing a double-throw switch into the circuit. Only I can trigger it. Thrown one way, you are cut out of the system. Thrown the other way, you are immersed totally into the system, your mortal body reduced permanently to the lowest level of subsistence."

"Spock. You can't let him do this to you."

"It appears I have no choice, Captain. I cannot resist, any more than you can."

"There must be something—"

"Quiet, Kirk," said the construct. "I am allowing you to live only so that you can see the results of this transfer. It should be interesting and informative to observe your reaction. Then you will be of no further use to me. However, if you continue with these persistent interruptions, I will be forced to kill you now."

Kirk fell silent, helpless.

The construct straightened up, looked pleased at its handiwork. "It is finished," it said, turning to insert the plug into the machine.

"No!" shouted Kirk, jumping to his feet. As the

construct grinned, he slumped to the floor. So much for that.

It slipped the plug into the receptable and Spock was one with the computer.

Scotty had tried to talk with Dr. McCoy a few minutes earlier, but had been informed McCoy was in the middle of an important experiment and could not be disturbed unless it was an emergency. Everything was an emergency, it seemed. But this could wait, at least for a little while.

He was concerned that they hadn't heard from the Captain or Mr. Spock. Nothing at all had come through. It was as if they had vanished. Vanished or . . .

He considered sending down a landing party, but what good would that do? If the Captain and Mr. Spock were in trouble, the crew could hardly help them. As it was, they would probably just be in the way.

Their best hope lay with Dr. McCoy and Dr. Davis, he was sure. But at last report, they were making no headway at all. At least Dr. McCoy hadn't sounded so depressed. Maybe they *could* do it. He had faith in the doctor, but this was a very tricky problem. Very tricky. For the thousandth time, he wished Mr. Spock was around.

"Still no word from the Captain, Mr. Scott," said Uhura. "And their Council is refusing to acknowledge calls."

Scotty nodded. He had a feeling in his bones that something significant was happening down there. He also felt it could come to no good.

CHAPTER FIFTEEN

First it was the velvety darkness, broken only by distant pinpoints of scattered light. The lights started to blink, shift. They looked very far away, moved around in random patterns that he almost believed he could control if he tried hard enough. He could hear the sound of crashing surf.

Spock immediately recognized the signs of sensory deprivation. His mind had been cut off from his body. Everything he felt, he felt through the computer. It was, to say the least, an unusual feeling.

Spock tried to bring it under control, failed. He tried again. It didn't work. With a conscious effort, he quit fighting it, just let it happen. It was like opening a door.

He became aware of jumbled inputs from a thousand different sources. Numbers and letters turned into electrical impulses and back into numbers and letters again. They made some degree of sense to him either way. He could even tell which electrical impulses were his own brain being monitored. Even as he watched, they sped away from him. He tried to move some data and was gently blocked. He realized that he was on probation, that he was limited by the construct in what he could do. He was like a child let loose in a playground, being told he could only use the slide, to stay away from the high swings. It was only the construct protecting itself.

He was aware of the presence of the construct. It existed as many lines running through the computer. It was woven into everything the computer did. It had a life of its own, but its nerves were buried deep in the data banks and a thousand other places, some accessible, others far away.

Spock searched for and found the switch that the construct had mentioned. It was not, as he had supposed, a physical switch. Rather, it was in the form of a part of the program that held Spock captive. It could only be thrown through the computer, not by external action. It was, of course, blocked from his access.

That switch was about the most logical thing Spock discovered. Years of interfacing with Wayne Perry had hopelessly tangled up the computer. Where there must have at one time been logic, now there was only confusion. It was unsettling. Subjective thoughts, distorted by time and age, bumped up against hard facts everywhere. It was a hopeless mess.

Then he opened another door, one he wished he had left shut. He found Wayne Perry.

Pain washed over him. Sharp pain, dull pain, pain that had lasted for hundreds of years. There was no relief to it. Each day was just like the one before it, the one after it, for as far back as Wayne Perry could remember. It colored everything. There was no bitterness, only remorse and resignation, buried in the red fog of unrelieved agony. Spock wanted to close the door, turn away. That would have been the easiest thing to do. Obviously, that was the course the construct had followed. Instead, Spock's mind worked its way deeper into the twisted, tortured anguish that was Wayne Perry. It was like falling into a hole.

A hole into hell.

Kirk stared at Spock's body on the slab. It seemed to him that life was being gradually drained from the Vulcan. His breathing was growing shallow. His eyes seemed focused on something far, far away.

"What have you done to him?" asked Kirk.

The construct turned away from the master console, where it had been making small adjustments. "He is being assimilated into the computer. Soon the process will be complete. He seems to be fitting well, functioning adequately within the constraints I set."

"You have no intention of removing him from the system, do you?"

"None whatsoever, Captain. I expect some resistance at first, but as long as he can do no harm, I can wait. After all, I have all the time in the world. Which is more than I can say for you." It raised the phaser once more.

"Your peace is stained with blood," said Kirk. "Spock would find that illogical."

"True enough," said the construct. "But that hardly bothers me. Any last words?"

"None for you."

"Stop!" Rus stepped through the door into the room. "You can't do this."

"Page Rus," said the construct. "You must leave."

"No."

"I order it."

"No. This is against the teachings. Violence can never be tolerated."

Rus was torn apart. This was not the side of Wayne Perry he had expected to find. Every bit of his upbringing had taught him to respect the man, what his eyes told him was much different.

"You do not understand what is happening. Leave at once."

Rus hesitated. Long-buried impulses churned within him. Violence was wrong. He had learned that from his mother, it had been reinforced with his every waking hour. Yet here was violence that could only be stopped by more violence. He wavered. Wayne Perry *had* to be wrong. He was about to take a life. That was never justified. He stepped forward. Firmly.

"So be it," said the construct. "I will kill you both." He swung the phaser around, activated it.

Ami screamed where she stood behind Rus, unseen until that moment.

Distracted, the construct's first shot went wild, striking the wall above Kirk's head. The wall, a portion of the computer, glowed red and exploded with a spray of sparks. Rus leaped at the construct, tackled it around the middle.

The next shot was blind, it skipped around the room. Everything it hit erupted with flaming destruction. It passed over the rigid body of Spock, struck the transparent dome containing the body of Wayne Perry. The resulting explosion rocked everyone in the room. Rus pinned the construct to the floor.

Through reflex or through desperation, the construct kept firing the phaser. It lapped toward the master console, held there. Black smoke and the crackle of electricity gone wild poured from the glowing control center. With a burst of blue fire it disintegrated. At that point, all the lights in the room went out, save the long-forgotten phosphorescent panels in the ceiling.

Quiet. Not even the hum of distant machinery. The sharp smell of ozone hung in the air.

Sobbing, Rus bent over the form of the construct, no longer human-appearing. The holographic enhancement had ceased along with all the other computer activities.

"What have I done?" he wept. "How could such a thing have happened?"

Kirk made his way through the smoke-filled dimness to the slab where Spock lay motionless. Is this how it ends, good friend? On such a rotten planet? Spock showed no signs of life.

"I'm sorry," said Rus. "I didn't know it would be this way."

"You did what you had to do," said Kirk.

"It turned out badly," he said.

"Not necessarily," said Spock. "It could, in the end, be beneficial."

In unison, they both turned to Spock, who was raising himself to a sitting position on the slab, removing the wires from his head.

"Spock," said Kirk. "I thought you were lost forever, gone with the computer."

"At the last moment I was set free, released from the interface."

"Don't tell me the construct let you go," said Kirk.

Spock pulled the last wire loose, shook his head. "No, Captain. The original Wayne Perry freed me. It was his last act."

"How . . . ?"

"I sought him out. Buried within the computer, he was in immeasurable pain and anguish. In a way I cannot explain, we melded. It was a very near approximation of the Vulcan mind-meld. I held nothing back from him, nor he from me. We touched each other. Deeply. He was a very troubled man, plagued by good ideas gone bad, noble experiments that had been twisted in a way he never intended. When the end came, he released me freely. He sought the end of his pain in the same way."

"He—he did live in two worlds," said Rus quietly.

"As I have lived all my life." He walked to Ami, who was slumped in the doorway. He held her, she opened her eyes.

"I saw it," she said. "There was violence. You did the unthinkable."

Rus stroked her hair, sadness in his eyes. "I have always tried to hide half my life. Now I know it is as much a part of me as the other half, the half you knew. I am ashamed."

"You shouldn't be," said Kirk. "You're no different, really, than all of us."

"How's that?" asked Rus.

"We all live in two worlds, in a balance between peace and violence, love and hate, yin and yang. For better or for worse, it is the human condition. We learn to live with it. We learn to strike a balance, to walk the middle line."

"I could never learn to do that."

"You will have to. You more than anyone."

Rus looked at him questioningly.

"Wayne Perry is dead, and along with him dies the society he tried to build. It has been decaying for years, and now it is finished. I doubt that there is much in this room that can be salvaged. There is probably little you would *want* to salvage. This is a fine planet, but it belongs to you, the people, not to Wayne Perry. Spread out. Live. Expand your horizons. That, too, is part of the human spirit."

"But what can *I* do?" asked Rus. "I am but a lowly page to the Council."

"Don't you see?" asked Kirk. "There is no more Council. Everything on this planet has been controlled by computer, now there is no more computer. The virus that has enslaved your people will someday be conquered. You, who have seen both sides of life on the planet, will be in the best position to help rebuild this world into a better place. You, and others like you."

"I know of no other one like me," said Rus.

"If you exist," said Spock, "then it is only logical to assume that others similar to you also exist. To survive, they have probably chosen, as you did, to bury their natural tendencies. They will come forward."

"You'll have your hands full," said Kirk. "The people have lived under the effects of the virus and the benevolent tyranny of Wayne Perry for a long time. It will be quite an adjustment."

"I don't think I'm capable of that."

"I think you are," said Kirk.

He looked at the body that had once been Wayne

Perry. If anything, it looked even older than it had before. It was dead, no doubt about it, dead after three hundred years. There was a smile on its face. Kirk could have sworn it wasn't there before.

"Let's go, Mr. Spock," he said quietly.

CHAPTER SIXTEEN

Scotty was more than glad to turn the ship back over to Captain Kirk. It had been a long and trying experience for the Scotsman, and he didn't care if he never sat in the Captain's chair again. He had a spanner in his hand and he was happy.

Kirk, on the other hand, was confused.

"Well, does it work, or doesn't it?" he asked.

"It *ought* to work," said McCoy, "but we don't know for sure. There's no way to test it except on a volunteer."

"So I volunteer," said Kirk.

McCoy shook his head. "I can't let you do that, Jim. That virus is the trickiest thing I've ever come across. It's intertwined so closely with the person's nervous system that even if it was removed there could be damage. Permanent damage." He held the spray hypo well away from Kirk.

"I am available," said Spock.

"No," said McCoy. "It might work differently on a Vulcan. Better to try it on a human first."

"That's illogical. The virus worked the same."

"You men could go on forever," said Kelly Davis. "You'll never get anywhere." She grabbed the spray hypo from McCoy's hand. Before anyone could stop her, she had injected herself in the arm.

"Kelly, no—"

"I know the risks, Dr. McCoy. I choose to take

them." She turned pale, staggered. Spock caught her, gave her support.

"It's got to be a jolt to her system," said McCoy. "It shouldn't last long, though. If it works or fails, we should know in a few moments."

"How do you feel, Dr. Davis?" asked Kirk.

"A little shaky, but fine otherwise."

"I would have done that," said Kirk.

"I know," said Kelly. "That's why I had to do it myself."

"Strike me," said Spock.

"What?" asked Kelly.

"Strike me. As hard as you wish."

"Isn't that out of character for you, Mr. Spock?" asked McCoy.

"I just wish to see if her inhibitions against violence have been removed. It is a valid method of inquiry."

Kelly Davis tapped Spock lightly on the arm. "I don't feel anything," she said. Then she hit him again, harder. Spock flinched in spite of himself. Kelly was in no way a weak woman.

"I think that will be sufficient," he said.

"It seems to work," said McCoy. "I'll just take Dr. Davis to sick bay and run her through a few tests. If everything checks out okay, I'll whip up enough of the cofactor to innoculate the crew. It's easy to prepare, once we figured it out. It shouldn't take very long at all."

"I want you to do me first," said Kirk.

"Of course, Jim. Any particular reason?"

"I have business to attend to. A score to settle."

Korol was not surprised when Captain Kirk materialized on the bridge. Everything else had gone wrong, why not this? The hate inside him welled up to the point where he grew dizzy, faint. He had to sit in the Commander's chair to keep from falling. He wished he had a sword in his hand. He wished he could use it if he had it. He wished . . . Impossible.

"What do you want, Earth-scum?" he asked. "Have you come to surrender? Again?"

"No, not to surrender. To avenge."

"What?" asked Korol.

"You are responsible for unprovoked attacks on a Federation ship. You caused the deaths of three of my crew and injury to others. Among other things you have violated the Organian Treaty, a treaty signed in good faith by both our representatives. For this you will be brought to trial and no doubt convicted."

"Murderer of my brother, I carry the blood oath on your head. Nothing shall stand in my way."

"Nothing?" asked Kirk. "Then why don't you take me now? I have no weapons." He walked over to the Commander's chair, stood directly in front of it, his hands outspread.

"You know as well as I that we are hamstrung by that insidious disease that fool of an engineer brought to us."

"I'm not," Kirk said evenly.

"What do you mean?" Korol asked, fear creeping into his voice.

"We have developed a cure for the virus," said Kirk. "I could take you apart with my bare hands."

"You wouldn't dare," said Korol in a quavering voice.

Kirk reached out, grabbed the Klingon by the shirt and dragged him to his feet. Their eyes met, inches apart. Kirk saw the hate in Korol's face turn to fear. He drew his right hand back.

Instead of striking Korol, he ripped the insignia from his shirt, threw them to the deck. He ground them under his foot.

"I have the capacity for violence," said Kirk, "but not the stomach for it."

Korol drew away in fear. Kirk shoved him back into the chair.

"At least your brother had courage, Korol. He may have been an enemy, but he was a man. That is more than I can say for you."

"Your day will come, Kirk."

"I don't doubt that, Korol. But not from you."

As he started to transport back to the *Enterprise*, Kirk felt nothing but relief. He had faced another one of his devils and purged it.

The priest entered his quarters without announcing himself. It was a breach of protocol of the most serious proportions.

"You have been shamed, Korol," he said without hesitation.

"What would you expect, old man? There is nothing I could have done."

"You have a mouth and a tongue, Korol. It is even assumed you have a mind to go with them. Had you used them, you would not be in disgrace."

"Words. *Hah*."

"With words you could have saved face. Instead you cringed, acted like the worst kind of coward. You have besmirched the good names of your father and brother. You do not deserve to be mentioned in the same breath with them."

"I was under the effects of the disease."

"That is no excuse. We all saw the Captain on the bridge. We saw you foul the names of your ancestors. I am breaking your blood oath. You are not fit to carry it out in the name of your brother."

"You can't do that!"

"As your priest, I most certainly can."

"That's only allowed under unusual circumstances."

"This is an unusual circumstance. You have no honor left to defend."

"You are a foul swine, old man."

"And you are a lost cause, ex-Commander Korol."

"Ex-Commander? What do you mean by that?"

"You have been relieved of command, as of this very moment. Your first officer is taking over. We are in the process of informing the High Command. No doubt they will not be pleased at your actions, particularly the loss of the sensor-evading device. They had great plans for that. I doubt they will have much patience with you."

"I have even less patience with you."

"That is of no concern to me, Korol. You have no hold over me, none at all. You are a shame to all Klingons."

"I wish upon you a most unpleasant death, priest."

The priest smiled. "I can almost assure you one, coward," he said as he walked out the door.

CHAPTER SEVENTEEN

Captain's Log, Stardate 6848.2:

We are awaiting the arrival of the U.S.S. *Phoenix* and Vice-Commodore Propp. They will relieve us of duty on this planet and we can proceed, at last, to Starbase 6. Their crew will remain here to oversee the initial restoration activities. Rus has shown remarkable talents in leadership, he should be an invaluable aid. These are strong people in spite of what has happened to them, and they are adapting very well. They have elected to receive the cofactor and that process will begin as soon as the *Phoenix* arrives. Kelly Davis will remain to aid their medical staff.

The cofactor that Dr. Davis and Dr. McCoy developed is remarkably effective. It has several unique properties and, ironically enough, shows some promise of being useful in treating Dexter's disease, along with other neurological disorders. Dr. McCoy has insisted that it be called the Davis Cofactor. He is emphatic that he could not have discovered it working on his own. We owe her a large debt.

Lieutenant Commander Scott's plan for infecting the Klingons was brilliant. He took a tremendous chance at great personal risk at a time when desperate measures were called for. Without him, the

Enterprise would surely have been lost. He is to be commended on his ingenuity.

As a matter of practicality, the Klingon ship remains infected with the virus. After the *Phoenix* arrives they will be given a supply of the cofactor. In the meantime, there is no sense in taking any chances.

The Klingon High Command has announced that Korol was acting entirely on his own and will be punished for his violation of the Organian Treaty. That's hardly news.

The *Phoenix* should arrive within the hour. It seems like we have been circling this planet for years.

Dr. McCoy brought Kelly Davis to the bridge. It was almost time for her to beam down with a supply of the cofactor.

"You know, Jim," he said, "this woman should be declared a national resource of the United Federation of Planets. She is an absolutely fantastic doctor."

"Oh, come on," said Kelly. "I'll bet you say that to all the girls."

McCoy grinned. "I'm offended," he said with mock indignation. "I meant every word of it."

"I don't detect an interest other than professional, do I, Bones?" asked Kirk.

"Come on, Jim. You know me better than that."

Kirk laughed. "You're just a dirty old man."

"And you're a washed-up tugboat captain."

"One thing is bothering this washed-up tugboat captain," said Kirk.

"Only one thing?" asked McCoy.

"Yes. When we were underground, I can understand how you put the guard to sleep, but I was wondering how in the world you managed to get that cell sample from him. You must have had to break the surface of the skin to do that. It had to hurt, even just a little. How did you manage that without the virus stopping you?"

"No problem at all, Jim. I've been telling people 'this won't hurt a bit' for so long, I actually believe it myself."

They laughed together. Kirk reached out and slapped McCoy playfully on the arm. McCoy stared at the place Kirk had hit. His smile grew larger. He hit Kirk back, a little harder. They exchanged light blows back and forth, laughing uproariously at having regained the freedom they once had lost.

Chekov and Sulu stared at each other. Had everyone gone mad? Then Chekov reached over, grinning, and mussed up Sulu's hair. Sulu roared and pushed Chekov out of his chair. Whooping and hollering with glee, they rolled around the deck of the bridge. It was infectious, everybody laughed, joined in with the merriment. Uhura went over and hugged Kelly. It felt good to feel good.

Only Spock seemed to be unaffected. He sat at his station, calmly watching the riotous behavior.

"Fascinating," he said. "Childish, but fascinating."

ABOUT THE AUTHOR

JACK C. HALDEMAN has for several years been entertaining the science fiction world with his short fiction. He is well known to people in the science fiction field as chairman of the World Science Fiction Convention in 1974. He is the elder brother of the well-known science fiction author Joe Haldeman and lives in Florida.

THE EXCITING REALM OF STAR TREK

THE TRIUMPHANT CONCLUSION
TO A MAGNIFICENT FANTASY TRILOGY

RAPHAEL

by R. A. MacAvoy

The stunning saga begun in DAMIANO and DAMI-
ANO'S LUTE concludes with this powerful volume.
Weakened by his contact with mortals, the Archangel
Raphael falls prey to his brother Lucifer, Prince of
Darkness, who strips him of his divinity. Sold in the
Moorish slave markets, confused and humbled by his
sudden humanity, Raphael finds his only solace in the
friendship of the dark-skinned Bedouin woman Djoura,
and the spiritual guardianship of his former pupil
Damiano Delstrego.

Accompanied by her rakish young friend Gaspare and
an ancient immortal black dragon, Damiano's beloved
Saara embarks on a quest to rescue Raphael. Their ody-
ssey leads them to a shattering confrontation with the
Father of Lies and a transcendent reckoning with destiny.

Buy RAPHAEL, and all of the works of R. A. MacAvoy,
on sale now wherever Bantam paperbacks are sold:

Beginning a galaxy-spanning saga
by the bestselling author of
THE WINDHOVER TAPES:

WARREN NORWOOD

THE DOUBLE SPIRAL WAR

Leaving behind their homeworld of Earth, the descendants of man set out across the dark ocean of space to find new worlds to conquer. There, centuries later, two mighty powers—the United Central Systems and the Sondak confederacy—clashed in a titanic struggle to control the stars.

VOLUME ONE:

MIDWAY BETWEEN

Strategically located halfway between the UCS and Sondak, the Matthews system commanded space in all directions. It was here, in the opening campaign of the war, that two old enemies met once again in a deadly dance of maneuver and counterstrike. And it was here that two young lovers were torn apart by the bitter winds of war....

"Grimly exciting ... it conveys a sense of a future and of other worlds that really are different from anything we know here and now."

—Poul Anderson

Don't miss MIDWAY BETWEEN, *available September 15, 1984,*
wherever Bantam Books are sold.